About Nikki Logan

Nikki Logan lives next to a string of protected wetlands in Western Australia, with her long-suffering partner and a menagerie of furred, feathered and scaly mates. She studied film and theatre at university, and worked for years in advertising and film distribution before finally settling down in the wildlife industry. Her romance with nature goes way back, and she considers her life charmed, given she works with wildlife by day and writes fiction by night— the perfect way to combine her two loves. Nikki believes that the passion and risk of falling in love are perfectly mirrored in the danger and beauty of wild places. Every romance she writes contains an element of nature, and if readers catch a waft of rich earth or the spray of wild ocean between the pages she knows her job is done.

TM

Once A Rebel...

Nikki Logan

Also by Nikki Logan

Mr Right at the Wrong Time
Rapunzel in New York
A Kiss to Seal the Deal
Shipwrecked with Mr Wrong
Lights, Camera…Kiss the Boss
Their Newborn Gift
Seven-Day Love Story
The Soldier's Untamed Heart
Friends to Forever

Did you know these are also available as eBooks?
Visit www.millsandboon.co.uk

For Tracy Scarparolo.
And to Dan, the best office-mate and friend
a girl could have.

PROLOGUE

www.remembermrsmarr.com
Front row seats for a Beethoven symphony
Bungee jump in New Zealand
Run a marathon
Ride like The Man from Snowy River
Hunt for a dinosaur fossil
Commune with the penguins in Antarctica
Float in a Hot Air Balloon
Climb the Sydney Harbour Bridge
Take a gondola ride in Venice
Climb Everest
Abseil down a cliff face
Be transported by a touch
Get up close and personal with dolphins
Take a cruise
Hold my grandchild

www.rem—
SHIRLEY keyed the first letters of the web address into her browser before it auto-completed the rest. She visited enough that it knew exactly where she wanted to go.

www.remembermrsmarr.com

The simple site opened and she spent the first moments—as she always did—staring at the face of her mother, captured forever in time in a delighted, head-thrown-back kind of joy. Exactly as she would have wanted people to see her. Exactly as her students did see her. And exactly how Shirley chose to re-member her now, with the benefit of distance.

Clicking through to the list she knew was on the next page only disappointed.

Still nothing in the first column—the one headed 'HT.'

After all this time.

Hayden Tennant had been her mother's all-time favourite student. He'd been the one—hurt and grieving—to suggest the tribute website in the first place. So that they could each do the items on her mother's bucket list. All the life experiences an unlicensed drunk-driver had robbed her of.

Hayden had pledged.

He'd *vowed* in that gorgeous, thick, grief-filled voice.

Yet every single square next to every single item on *www.remembermrsmarr.com* was empty where Hayden's ini-tials should have been.

Today was an extra sucky day to be staring at the list and finding it empty. Because today was ten years since Carol-Anne Marr had taken her last breath. How many weeks had passed before he'd forgotten all about it? Or was it days? Hours? Did he think no one would notice? Did he think his teacher's only daughter wouldn't be watching? Shirley tapped her purple fin-gernails on the keyboard and enjoyed the sound of the slick keys under them.

Come on, Hayden. You've had a decade.

Something.

Anything.

Swimming with dolphins. Climbing the Harbour Bridge. Running a marathon. Even *she'd* done that one, back before she'd got boobs. Back when her schedule had been able to tol-erate training for eight straight hours. It had taken her eighteen months to train up and get old enough to qualify, but then she'd placed in the middle of the under-sixteens category and held her medal to the heavens as she lurched across the finish line.

And then she'd never run again.

If I can tick that one off, surely you can, Tennant.

Hayden, with his long, fast legs. His intense focus. His rigid determination. He wouldn't even need to train, he'd just *will* himself to last the entire forty-two kilometres.

She'd hoped for a while that he was honouring her mother privately, keeping his own list the way she herself was.

But the truth had finally dawned.

All that angst, all that sorrow and despair at her funeral; all of that was simply the emotion of the moment. Like a performance piece. Terribly dramatic and intense. Terribly Hayden. None of it had been genuine. Amazing, really, that he was still forking out the cash annually to maintain the domain name.

She cocked her head.

The domain...

It took her just a few minutes to track down the site registration details and a few more for a contact number for the company it was registered to. Molon Labe Enterprises. That had to be him. He'd had a thing for Spartans the entire time she'd known him.

Known *of* him.

Watched him.

She chased down the contact details for the company right here in Sydney and its executive structure. He wasn't on it. Disappointed by that dead end, she called the company direct and asked for him outright.

'Mr Tennant does not take calls,' the receptionist told her.

Really? Too busy and important? 'Could you give me his email address, please?'

It took the officious woman nearly a minute to outline all the reasons why she couldn't. Shirley rang off, far from defeated. Chasing down story leads was what she did for a living. It wasn't stalking if you were a professional. A bit of reconnaissance, finding out where he was and what was so important it had made him forget the promises of a decade ago...

That was doable. He'd never even know.

Thank goodness for search engines.

Two hours went by before she surfaced, frowning deeply at the screen. Hayden Tennant was a time bomb. Her online search was littered with images of him stumbling out of one seedy venue or another on the arm of some blonde—always a blonde—going back six years. In most of them, it was hard to tell who was holding up whom, but the club security was always on hand to facilitate their departure.

She stared at one image. He looked nothing like the Hayden she remembered. He used to get around in a shabby kind of hip style—*the garret look,* her mother had used to joke and make Shirley promise never to go out in public like that. So of course she had instantly wanted to. The designer lank hair, holed jumper and frequently bare feet. Bohemian plus. She'd coveted everything about his personal style back then, as only a love-sick fourteen-year-old could.

But the Internet had him in some pretty fancy threads now, as carefully fitted as the women accessorising the sharp suit and cars.

Guess everyone grows up.

She searched up Molon Labe's website, flicked through to their corporate contacts and scribbled down the address. Maybe his reception staff would find it harder to say no to her face? Not that she had the vaguest idea of what she'd say if she saw him.

Or why she wanted to.

Maybe so she could ask him, personally, why he hadn't bothered to tick a single box. Maybe because she owed it to her mother.

Or maybe just so she could finally nail a lid on the last remnants of her childhood.

CHAPTER ONE

'PLEASE be a stripper.'

His voice was thick and groggy, as though she'd just roused him from sleep. Maybe she had. It was a gently warm and breezeless day and Hayden Tennant looked as if he'd been lying in that longish grass at the base of the slope behind his cottage for quite some time.

Shirley found some air and forced it past a larynx choked with nerves. This suddenly seemed like a spectacularly bad idea.

'Were you expecting one?' she breathed.

He scrutinised her from behind expensive sunglasses. 'No. But I've learned never to question the benevolence of the universe.'

Still so fast with a comeback. The man in front of her might have matured in ways she hadn't anticipated but he was still *Hayden* inside.

Somewhere.

She straightened and worked hard not to pluck at her black dress. It was the tamest thing in her wardrobe. 'I'm not a stripper.'

His head flopped back down onto the earth and his eyes closed again. 'That's disappointing.'

Discharged.

She stood her ground and channelled her inner Shiloh. She wouldn't let his obvious dismissal rile her. Silent minutes ticked by. His long body sprawled comfortably where he lay. She took the opportunity to look him over. Still lean, still all legs. A tiny, tidy strip of facial hair above his lip and on his chin. Barely there but properly manicured. It only half-covered the scar she knew marred his upper lip.

The biggest difference was his hair. Shorter now than when he'd been at uni and a darker blond. It looked as if someone who knew what they were doing had cut it originally, but she guessed they hadn't had a chance to provide any maintenance recently.

She pressed her lips together and glared pointlessly at him as the silence continued. Had he gone back to sleep?

'I can do this all day,' he murmured, eyes still closed. 'I have nowhere to be.'

She spread her weight more evenly on her knee-high boots and appreciated every extra inch they gave her. 'Me, too.'

He lifted his head again and opened his eyes a crack.

'If you're not here to give me a lap dance, what do you want?'

Charming. 'To ask you some questions.'

He went dangerously still. Even the grass seemed to stop its swaying. 'Are you a journalist?'

'Not really.'

'It's a yes/no question.'

'I write for an online blog.' *Understatement.* 'But I'm not here in that capacity.'

He pulled himself up and braced against one strong arm in the turf. Did that mean she had his attention?

'How did you find me?'

'*Molon Labe.*'

He frowned and lifted his sunglasses to get a better look at her. His eyes were exactly as blue and exactly as intense as she remembered. She sneaked in a quick extra breath.

'My office wouldn't have given you this address.'

No. Not even face to face.

'I researched it.' Code for *I stalked your offices.*

It had taken a few visits to the coffee shop over the road to spot what messenger company they used most regularly. A man at the head of a corporation he didn't visit had to get documents delivered to wherever he was, right? For signatures at least. Sadly for them, if Hayden ever found out, the courier company had been only too obliging when a woman purporting to be from Molon Labe had called to verify the most recent details of one of their most common delivery addresses.

His eyes narrowed. 'But you're not here in a journalistic capacity?'

'I'm not a journalist.'

'Or a stripper, apparently.' He glanced over her from foot to head. 'Though that seems wasted.'

She forced herself not to react. She'd chosen this particular outfit carefully—knee-high boots, black scoop-neck dress cinched at the waist and falling to her knees—but she'd been going more for *I am woman* and less for *I am pole dancer.*

'You used to say sarcasm was the lowest form of wit,' she murmured.

One eye narrowed, but he gave no other sign of being surprised that she already knew him. 'Actually, someone else did. I just borrowed it. I've come to be quite fond of sarcasm in the years since...?' He left it open for her to finish the sentence.

He didn't recognise her.

Not entirely surprising, given how different she must have looked when he last saw her. Fourteen, stick-insect-thin, mousy, uninspired hair. A kid. She hadn't discovered fashion—and her particular brand of fashion—until she was sixteen and her curves had busted out.

'You knew my mother,' she offered carefully.

The eyes narrowed again and he pushed himself to his feet. Now it was his turn to tower over her. It gave him a great view down her scoop neck and he took full advantage. His eyes eventually came back to hers.

'I may have been an early starter but I think it's a stretch to suggest I could be your father, don't you?'

Hilarious.

'Carol-Anne Marr,' she persisted, the name itself an accusation.

Was it wrong that she took pleasure from the flash of pain he wasn't quite fast enough to disguise? That she grasped so gratefully at any hint of a sign that he hadn't forgotten her mother the moment she was in the ground. That he wasn't quite as faith-less as she feared.

'Shirley?' he whispered.

And it *had* to be wrong how deeply satisfied she felt that he even knew her name. Hayden Tennant wasn't a god; if he ever had been he was well and truly fallen now. But still her skin tingled.

She lifted her chin. 'Shiloh.'

His eyes narrowed. 'Shiloh?'

'It's what I go by now.'

The blue in his eyes greyed over with disdain. 'I'm not call-ing you Shiloh. What's wrong with Shirley—not hip enough for you?'

It killed her that he was still astute enough to immediately put himself in the vicinity of the secret truth. And that she was still foolish enough to admire that. 'I preferred something that was more...me.'

'Shirley means "bright meadow".'

Exactly. And she, with her raven hair and kohl-smudged eyes, was neither bright nor meadow-like. 'Shiloh means "gift". Why can't it be a gift to myself?'

'Because your mother already gifted you a name. Changing it dishonours her.'

Tendrils of unexpected hurt twisted in her gut and rolled into a tight, cold ball and pushed up through her ribcage. But she swallowed it back and chose her words super-carefully. 'You're criticising *me* for not honouring her?'

Surprise and something else flooded his expression. Was that regret? Guilt? Confusion? None of those things looked right on a face normally filled with arrogant confidence. But it didn't stay long; he replaced it with a careless disinterest. 'Something you want to say, Shirley?'

Suddenly presented with the perfect opportunity to close that chapter on her life, she found herself speechless. She glared at him instead.

He shook his head. 'For someone who doesn't know me, you don't like me very much.'

'I know you. Very well.'

He narrowed one eye. 'We've never met.'

Actually they had, but clearly it wasn't memorable. Plus, she'd participated secretly in every gathering her mother had hosted in their home. Saturday extra credit for enthusiastic students. Hayden Tennant had been at every one.

'I know you through my mother.'

His lush lips tightened. She'd always wondered if her own fixation with Lord Byron had something to do with the fact that in her mind he shared Hayden's features. Full lips, broad forehead, intense eyes under a serious brow... Byron may have preceded him in history but Hayden came first in *her* history.

'If you're suggesting your mother didn't like me I'm going to have to respectfully disagree.'

'She adored you.' *So did her daughter, but that's beside the point.* She took a deep breath. 'That makes what you've done doubly awful.'

His brows drew down. 'What I've done?'

'Or what you haven't done.' She stared, waiting for the penny-drop that never came. For such a bright man, he'd become very obtuse. 'Does *remembermrsmarr.com* ring any bells?'

His face hardened. 'The list.'

'The list.'

'You're 172.16.254.1'

'What?'

'Your IP address. I get statistics from that website. I wondered who was visiting it so often.'

'I...' How had this suddenly become about her? And why was he monitoring visitation on a website he'd lost interest in almost immediately after he had set it up? It didn't fit with the man she visualised who had forgotten the list by the time the funeral bill came in.

'I visit often,' she said.

'I know. At least three times a week. What are you waiting for?'

She sucked in a huge breath and ignored the flick of his eyes down to her rising cleavage. 'I'm waiting for you to tick something.'

An eternity passed as he stared at her, the sharp curiosity he'd always had for everything in life dulling down to a careful nothing. 'Is that why you're here? To find out why I haven't ticked some box?'

Pressing her lips together flared her nostrils. 'Not just some box. *Her* box. My mother's dying wishes. The things you were supposed to finish for her.'

His eyes dropped away for a moment and when they lifted again they were softer. Kinder. So much worse. 'Shirley, look—'

'Shiloh.'

'*Shirley*. There's a whole bunch of reasons I haven't been able to progress your mother's list.'

'"Progress" suggests you've actually started.' Okay, now she was being as rude as he'd been on her arrival. Her high moral ground was crumbling. She lifted her chin. 'I came because I wanted to know what happened. You were so gutted at the funeral, how could you have followed through on none of them?'

He shrugged. 'Real life got in the way.'

Funny. Losing your mother at fourteen had felt pretty real to her. 'For ten years?'

His eyes darkened. 'I don't owe you any explanation, Shirley.'

'You owe her. And I'm here in her place.'

'The teacher I knew never would have asked anyone to justify themselves.'

He pushed past her and headed for his house. She turned her head back over her shoulder. 'Was she so easily forgotten, Hayden?'

Behind her, his crunching footfalls on the path paused. His voice, when it came, was frosty. 'Go home, Shirley. Take your high expectations and your bruised feelings and your do-me boots and get back in your car. There's nothing for you here.'

She stood on the spot until she heard the front door to his little cottage slam shut. Disappointment washed through her. Then she spun and marched up the path towards her car, dress swishing.

But as she got to the place where the path forked, her steps faltered.

Go home was not an answer. And she'd come for answers. She owed it to her mother to at least try to find out what had happened. To put this particular demon to rest. She stared at the path. Right led to the street and her beaten-up old car. Left led to the front door of Hayden's secluded cottage.

Where she and her opinions weren't welcome.

Then again, she'd made rather a life speciality out of unpopular opinions. Why stop now?

She turned left.

Hayden marched past his living room, heading for the kitchen and the hot pot of coffee that substituted for alcohol these days. But, as he did so, he caught sight of a pale figure, upright and prim on his lounge-room sofa. Like a ghost from his past.

He backed up three steps and lifted a brow at Shirley through the doorway.

'Come in.'

Her boots were one thing when she was standing, but seated and carefully centred, and with her hands and dress demurely folded over the top of them, they stole focus, big time. Almost as if the more modest she tried to be, the dirtier those boots got. He wrestled with his gaze to prevent it following his filthy mind. This was Carol-Anne's kid.

Though there was nothing kid-like about her now.

'The door was unlocked.'

'Obviously.'

She pressed her hands closer together in her lap. 'And I wasn't finished.'

'Obviously.'

Less was definitely more with this one. The women he was used to being with either didn't understand half of what he said or they were smart enough not to try to keep up. It had been a long time since he'd got as good as he'd given. One part of him hankered for a bit of intellectual sparring. Another part of him wanted to run a mile.

'I think you should finish the list,' she said in a clear, brave voice.

Little faker.

'Start the list, technically.'

'Right.' She seemed nonplussed that he'd made a joke about it. Was she expecting him to go on the attack? Where was the fun in that when he could toy with her longer by staying cool?

Now that he looked at her, he could see the resemblance to Carol under all her make-up. *Mrs Marr* to everyone else, but he'd presumed to call her Carol the first time he'd sat in her class and she'd smiled every time and never corrected him.

It was Shirley's irises that were like her mother's—the palest khaki. He'd have assumed contact lenses if not for the fact that he'd seen them before on a woman too sensible and too smart to be sucked in by the trappings of vanity. Shirley reminded him of one of those Russian dolls-inside-a-doll things. She had large black pupils surrounded by extraordinary grey-green irises, within the clearest white eyeballs he'd ever seen, and the whole thing fringed by smudges of catwalk charcoal around her lashes. Her eyes were set off by ivory skin and the whole picture was framed by a tumble of black locks piled on top. Probably kept in place by some kind of hidden engineering, but it looked effortless enough to make him want to thrust his hands into it and send it tumbling down.

Just to throw her off her game.

Just to see how it felt sliding through his fingers.

Instead, he played the bastard. The last time he'd seen her she'd been standing small and alone at her mother's funeral, all bones and unrealised potential. Now she was... He dropped his gaze to the curve of her neck. It was only slightly less gratuitous than staring at her cleavage.

Another thing he hadn't touched in years. Curves.

'Looks like you've been on good pasture.'

The only sign of that particular missile hitting its target was the barest of flinches in her otherwise steady gaze. She swallowed carefully before speaking and sat up taller, expression composed. 'You really work hard at being unpleasant, don't you?'

A fighter. Good for her.

He shrugged. 'I am unpleasant.'

'Alcohol does that.'

His whole body froze. *A dirty fighter, then.* But his past wasn't all that hard to expose with a few hours and an Internet connection. 'I don't drink any more.'

'Probably just as well. Imagine how unbearable you'd be if you did.'

He fixed his eyes on her wide, clear ones, forcing his mind not to find this verbal swordplay stimulating. 'What do you want, Shirley?'

'I want to ask you about my mother.'

'No, you don't. You want to ask me about the list.'

'Yes.' She stared, serene and composed. The calmness under pressure reminded him a lot of her mother.

'How did you even know it existed?'

Her steady eyes flicked for just a moment. 'I heard you, at the wake. Talking about it.'

He'd not let himself think about that day in a long, long time. 'Why didn't you add your name?'

She shrugged. 'I wasn't invited.' Her eyes dropped. 'And I didn't even know she had a bucket list until that day.'

Did that hurt her? That her mother had shared it with strangers but not her? A long dormant part of him lifted its drowsy head. Empathy. 'You were young. We were her peers.'

She snorted. 'You were her students.'

The old criticism still found a target. Even after all this time. 'You weren't there, Shirley. We were more like friends.' He had hungered for intellectual stimulation he just hadn't found in students his own age and her mother had filled it.

'I was there. You just didn't know it.'

He frowned. 'What do you mean?'

'I used to hide under the stairs when you would all come over for your extra credit Saturdays. Listen in. Learn.'

What? 'You were, what, fourteen?'

'Actually, I was eleven when you first started coming. I was fourteen when you stopped.'

'Most eleven-year-olds don't have a fascination with phi-losophy.'

She licked her lips, but otherwise her face remained carefully neutral. Except for the tiny flush that spiked high in her cheeks. And he knew she was lying about something.

'Ask me what you really want to know.' *And then go.* His tolerance for company was usually only as long as it took to get laid.

She leaned forward. 'Why didn't you even start the list?'

Oh…so many reasons. None of them good and none of them public. 'How many have *you* done?' he asked instead.

'Six.'

Huh. That was a pretty good rate, given she had been a teen-ager for the first half of that decade. The old guilt nipped. 'Which ones?'

'Ballooning, horse-riding in the Snowy Mountains, mara-thon—'

He gave her curves a quick once-over. 'You ran a marathon?' She ignored him. With good reason.

'—abseiling, and climbing the Harbour Bridge.'

The easy end of the list. 'That's only five.'

'Tomorrow I swim with the dolphins.'

Tomorrow. The day after today. Something about the imme-diacy of that made him nervous. 'Won't you eviscerate if you go in the sun, or something?'

She glared at him. 'I'm pale, I'm not a vampire. Stop hedg-ing. Why haven't you done a single one?'

She was going to keep on asking until he told her. And she wasn't going to like the answer. 'I've been too busy besmirch-ing my soul.'

She frowned. 'Meaning?'

'Making lots of money.'

'That should make it easier to do the things on the list, not harder.'

'Success doesn't make itself. You have to work hard. Put in the hours.' So many hours…

Her lips thinned. 'I'm well aware of that. But this list was your idea. To remind you of the importance of feeding your soul.' His own words sounded pretentious on her dark-red lips. 'To honour my mother's memory.'

The distress she was trying to hide under her anti-tan crept out in the slightest of wobbles.

There it was again. The weird pang of empathy. 'They're meaningless, Shirley. The things. They won't bring her back.'

'They keep her alive. In here.' Pressing her long, elegant fingers to her sternum only highlighted the way her dress struggled to contain her chest. And the way her chest struggled to contain her anger.

'That's important for *you*; you're her daughter—'

'You were her friend.'

His gut screwed down into a hard fist. He pushed to his feet. Forced lightness to his voice. 'What are you, the Ghost of Christmas Past? Life goes on.'

Those eyes that had seemed big outside were enormous in here, under the fluorescent glow of her sorrow. The silence was breached only by the sound of her strained breathing.

'What happened to you, Hayden?' she whispered.

He flinched. 'Nothing.'

'I believed you, back then. When you sat at my mother's funeral looking so torn up and pledged to honour her memory.'

She stared at him. Hard. As if she could see right through him. And for one crazy moment he wished that were true. That someone could drag it all out into the open to air. Instead of festering. But the rotting had started long before he'd begun to go to her house on Saturdays.

He clenched his fists behind his back. 'That makes two of us.'

'It's not too late to start.'

He needed to be moving. 'Oh, I think the time for me to make good on that particular promise is long past,' he said, turning and walking out of the room.

She caught up with him in the kitchen, grabbed his arm and then dropped it just as quickly. Did she feel the same jolt he had?

Her steady words gave nothing away. 'Come to the dolphins with me tomorrow.'

'No.'

She curled the fingers she'd touched him with down by her side. 'Why not? Scared?'

He turned and gave her his most withering stare. 'Please.'

'Then come.'

'Not interested.'

The smile she threw him was tight, but not unattractive. 'I'll drive.'

He glanced down at her boots. 'You're just as likely to get your heel speared in the accelerator and drive us into—'

At the very last moment, his brain caught up with his mouth. She didn't need a reminder of how her mother had died.

Silence weighed heavily.

She finally broke it. 'I'll pick you up at dawn.'

'I won't be here,' he lied. As if he had anywhere else to be.

'I'll come anyway.' She turned for the door.

He shouted after her. 'Shirley—'

'Shiloh.'

'—why are you doing this?'

She paused, but didn't turn back. He had no trouble hearing her, thanks to the hallway's tall ceiling. 'Because it's something I *can* do.'

'She won't know,' he murmured.

Her shoulders rose and fell. Just once.

'No. But I will.' She started down the hall again. 'And so will you.'

CHAPTER TWO

'COME on, Hayden,' Shirley muttered.

She banged the door with the heel of her hand to protect her acrylics. She paused, listened. Stepped back and leaned over to look in the window.

Which bothered her more? The fact that he'd actually left his home before dawn to avoid having to see her again or the fact that she could have turned around a dozen times on the drive over here—maybe should have—but she'd decided not to.

Because she wanted to give him a chance. The old Hayden.

No one could be *that much* of an ass, surely. She stared at the still silent door.

Looked as if he was the real deal.

'Ass!' she yelled out to the empty miles around them, then turned and walked away.

The front door rattled as her foot hit the bottom step on his porch.

'Is that some kind of greeting ritual in your culture?'

By the time she had turned, Hayden was leaning on the door-frame. Shirtless, barefoot. A pair of green track pants hanging low on his hips and bunched at his ankles. Looking for all the world like he wasn't expecting a soul.

One hundred per cent intentional.

He was trying to throw her.

'Good. You're ready,' she breezed, working hard to keep her breathing on the charts and her eyes off his bare chest. She'd spent years as a teenager secretly imagining what her mother's star pupil would look like under all his loose bohemian layers. The sudden answer may not have been what her teenage self would have conceived, but it didn't disappoint. No gratuitous muscle-stacks, just the gently curved contours up top and the long, angular lines down lower that showed he kept himself in good, lean shape.

And he knew it.

She fixed a brave smile on her face and turned to make room for him on the steps. 'Shall we?'

'You don't actually think I'm going like this?' he drawled.

No. She hadn't. But she'd be damned if she'd play his games. She kept her face impassive. 'Depends if you have swimmers on beneath the track pants.'

His grin broadened, dangerously good for this early in the morning. 'Nope. Nothing at all under these.'

Her pulse kicked into gear. But she fought it. 'Well, you'll have to change.'

'Easily offended, Shirley?' He dropped his chin so that he peered up at her across long, dark lashes. It was possibly the sexiest thing she'd ever seen. More theatrics. She took a breath and remembered who she was. And who Shiloh had dealt with and bested in the past.

'The dolphins.' She lifted her chin. 'Wouldn't want them to mistake you for a bait fish.'

An awful tense silence crackled between them and Shirley wondered if she'd gone a step too far. But then he tipped his head far back and laughed.

'Give me five...' he said, still chuckling, and was gone.

She let her breath out slowly and carefully. That could easily have gone the other way. Maybe the last ten years hadn't thoroughly ruined him, then.

Only partly.

When he returned he was more appropriately clothed in a T-shirt, sports cap, board shorts and sockless runners. The covered-up chest was a loss but at least she could concentrate on the road with him fully clothed. The T-shirt sleeves half covered a tattoo on his biceps, but she'd been able to read it briefly as he stretched his arm up the doorframe earlier.

MΩΛΩN ΛABE. Classical Greek.

She turned for the street.

'I'm not getting in that.' His arms crossed and his expression was implacable.

'Why not?'

He eyed her car. 'This looks like the floor might fall out of it if you put a second person in it. We'll take my Porsche.'

Nope. 'Wouldn't be seen dead in it. This is a '59 Karmann Ghia. Your Porsche's ancestor.'

'It's purple.'

'Well spotted. Get in.'

'And it has Shiloh plates.'

'And here I thought your mind was more lint-trap than steel-trap these days.'

He glared at her. 'I'm not driving this.'

She snorted. 'You're not driving at all.'

'Well, you're sure as hell not.'

She swallowed the umbrage. 'Because…?'

'Because *I* drive me.'

'You had a chauffeur.' She'd seen him in enough Internet photos falling out of limos or back into them.

'That's different.'

'You're welcome to ride in the back seat if it will make you feel more at home.' *And if you can dislocate your hips to squeeze in there.*

He glared at the tiny back seat and came to much the same conclusion. 'I don't think so.'

He folded himself into her low passenger seat and turned to stare as she tucked the folds of her voluminous skirt in under the steering wheel.

'Not the most practical choice for swimming, I would have thought,' he challenged.

'It won't be getting wet.'

His eyes narrowed. 'Because we won't or because you have something else?'

She glanced at him, then away. 'I have something else.' A something else she never would have worn in a million years if she'd had more than a few hours' notice that he was coming along. In fact, she would have chosen a totally different box on her mother's list if she'd thought for a moment that Hayden would actually join her. Something that didn't involve taking anything off. She'd only asked him along to shake him out of the unhappy place she'd found him. And to get him started on the list.

But parading around in swimwear in the presence of the man who'd made such a crack about her curves—yet who was apparently fixated by them—was not high on her list of most desirable things.

The thirty-minute drive would have been a whole heap more enjoyable if she'd been able to sing to the music pumping out of the phone docked to her stereo. It did prevent much in the way of conversation—a bonus—though it contributed to Hayden's general surliness—a minus—even after she'd pulled into a coffee drive-through for him. He'd leaned across her to take the coffee from the drive-through window and the brush of his shoulder, the heat of his body and the scent of early-morning man had stayed with her for the rest of the drive. She left her window wound down in the vain hope that the strong salty breeze would blow the distracting masculine fog away.

When they arrived at the beach, Hayden found himself a comfortable spot in the shade to resume napping and she wandered off to change in the public changing rooms.

She peeled off her dark red skirt, top and sandals, stored them carefully in her temporary locker and glanced critically in the mirror at what remained. Black one-piece, sheer wrap-around skirt—also black—purple and black striped stockings to her mid thighs.

Swimwear for the undead. If the undead ever went to the beach.

She piled her hair high, smoothed thirty-plus-plus-plus foundation where her neck was suddenly exposed and turned to the mirror.

Pretty good. Nothing she could do about the Boadicean body.

She'd had it since she was sixteen and had learned by necessity to love it, even if it wasn't apparently to the taste of a man more used to size zero. But she still looked like Shiloh. And Shiloh could definitely walk out onto that beach and spend a morning in the water with Hayden Tennant.

Even if Shirley wasn't certain she could.

Today wasn't about how good or otherwise she looked in a swimsuit, and it wasn't even about the man waiting outside the changing rooms. Today was about living another experience that her mother had never had the chance to.

Making good on her promise to her fourteen-year-old self.

She swung away from the mirror and stepped through the door into the light.

'What were you doing, sewing the—' His impatient words dried up when he saw her, his mouth frozen half-open. The fascination in his gaze should have annoyed her, not made her pulse jog.

Not everyone appreciated her fashion sense. She understood that. And she got *that* look a dozen times a day. But somehow on Hayden it rankled extra much.

She walked towards him and retrieved her towel. 'Ready to go?'

'You can't... Can you swim in that?' he muddled.

'I'm not expecting to swim, just wade. The dolphins will come to us.' A blessing, because waist-high water would disguise her worst assets and highlight her best. And the dolphins below the water wouldn't care about her sporting thighs.

It didn't take Hayden long to recover his composure and he followed her down to the water's edge, glancing sideways at her and smiling enigmatically. She kept her chin high the entire way, ready for another crack about her body.

None came.

She smiled at the girl working at the edge of the water and breezed, 'Hi, I'm—'

'I know who you are,' the teenager gushed, ticking off her name on her register. 'I couldn't believe it when I saw who was in today.'

Hayden glanced from her to the young girl and back again. Confused. Small revenge for how off-kilter he'd tried to keep her yesterday.

'I'm looking forward to it.' Shirley smiled. 'What do we do?'

The girl stammered less when she was in official mode and so their instructions were quick. Head right out into the low tide, where a distant volunteer was waiting for them, and then stand still when the dolphins come.

Simple.

But not for Hayden. He stood rooted to the spot as she waded ahead of him into the surf, stockings and all.

She turned and looked back at him, the slight waves buffeting her. 'Coming?'

Or was he going to bail?

His eyes narrowed and he slid his sunglasses down against the glare of the water, then followed her out.

His longer strides meant they reached the volunteer at the same time. The man launched straight into a security drill, although the only emergency they really ever had was if the dolphins got too boisterous and knocked someone down. Then he opened a pouch on his side and retrieved a defrosted treat.

'Bait fish,' he announced as he held it under the surface and shook the morsel.

Shirley glanced sideways at Hayden, who was concentrating in the same direction as the volunteer. Except he had the tiniest of smiles on his lips. Exactly the same size as hers.

Within minutes, they found themselves circled by three curious dolphins.

'They come in every day about this time,' the man told them. 'And in the afternoon too, in summer. Three, sometimes more.'

Shirley held her footing against the repeated close buffeting of the soft warm mammals. Hayden did the same.

'They're well trained,' he commented.

'Not trained. They come in because they want to. We just make sure we're standing in the right spot when they come.'

Hayden's snort could have been a puff of air as one of the

larger males ran up against him. 'It has nothing to do with the fish you were waving around.'

Shirley glanced at him. *Really?* He was going to be like this? When they were here in her mother's name?

'We only use one fish to encourage them over. We don't want them to get habituated,' the man said.

'Yep. That would be awful for your business,' Hayden murmured below his breath.

'They stay because they want to.' The volunteer held his own. 'They find us interesting. This is their routine, not ours. We just bring people here to meet them.'

'Yet you charge for the privilege?'

'Hayden,' she muttered. 'Do you remember why we're here? Can you contain your cynicism for a few minutes, please?'

But the volunteer didn't need her help. He stood taller. 'Twenty-eight dollars of your entry fee goes directly to cetacean research. The other two dollars helps pay our wildlife licences and fees. All our staffing is volunteer-based.'

'What would stop me from walking up the beach this time tomorrow and waving my own fish?'

Shirley pressed her lips together.

'Nothing at all,' the man confessed. 'Except that here you'll learn a whole heap more about these amazing creatures than just how much they like fish.'

Hayden stood straighter and considered that.

Heh. *Volunteer: one... Bitter, twisted cynic: nil.*

'What sort of things?' she asked, moving the man on and giving him her best Shiloh.

Amazing things, was the answer.

He plied them with stories of dolphin intelligence and resilience and sentience and even unexplainable, extra-sensory experiences, and all the while the dolphins wove in between them, trying to trip them up, playing with each other.

'My colleague, Jennifer, had worked here four years and then one day Rhoomba, the big male—' he pointed at one of the dolphins '—started to nudge her mid-section. Every day he'd shove his snout just under her ribs and stare there intently. He got quite obsessed. One of the old fishermen who knows these waters told her to go for tests. They found a tumour behind her liver. She was away from the beach for over a year with the surgery and her chemo but on her first time back Rhoomba nudged her once, just to check, and then never did it again.'

Hayden lifted just one eyebrow over the rim of his sunglasses. Shirley hurried to fill the silence before he said something unpleasant.

'How is she now?'

'Good as gold. No further problems.'

They spent fifteen minutes out in the water, even after the dolphins swam off to re-join their pod. Volunteer talking, Shirley questioning, Hayden glowering. But the chill coming off the water finally got their attention.

'Make sure you give us a good rap, Shiloh,' the volunteer said, winding up.

'No question,' she assured. 'It was amazing, thank you so much.'

He turned for shore. So did Hayden.

He had taken a few steps before he realised she wasn't following. 'Shirley?'

'I'll be a sec.' She let the onshore breeze carry her words back to him and she stared out into the sea where the dolphins now swam deep. The rhythmic slosh of the waves against her middle was hypnotic. Hairs blew loose from the pile atop her head and flew around her face.

'Another one done, Mum,' she murmured to the vast nothingness of the sea after a moment. 'I would have preferred to do this with you, instead of—' She cut herself off. 'But it's a start, hey?'

There was no response save the beautiful language of air rushing across water. It was answer enough.

Then right behind her, a voice spoke, cold and curious. And male.

'Why exactly are you so determined to make me start this list?'

* * *

I would have preferred to do this with you, instead of—

Him.

If there was any doubt in his mind as to what she meant, it evaporated the moment Shirley spun her horrified face to his. It was more ashen than usual.

'I thought you'd gone in.' Flummoxed. Discomposed. The only sign he'd had of the real person beneath the make-up since the barest eyelid flinch yesterday.

'I bet you did.'

But she didn't answer his question. She just started pushing towards shore, hurrying ahead of him. He gave her a few moments, mostly enjoying the view as the sea floor rose to become the shore and first revealed the curve of her sodden wraparound skirt and then those ridiculous stockings. Except they weren't entirely ridiculous; they were also one part intriguing. The way they clung just above her knee. It made the narrow strip of skin above the stocking but below the wrap into something really tantalising. Even though there was much more gratuitous flesh on show higher up.

This was forbidden.

This was private.

And, from the back, it was insanely hot, because even *she* didn't get to see that angle.

He took his time following her as his cells blazed.

Onshore, she retrieved her towel and turned back to him, clutching it to her body. It did a reasonable job of helping him focus.

Down the sand, the teenage girl who'd gushed earlier called out, 'Bye, Shiloh!', as if they were now best friends. Shirley threw her a dazzling smile in return and waved, making her day.

Gracious.

He should have expected that of a Marr.

The brilliant smile looked out of place with lips coloured like black blood, but he realised that somewhere between yesterday and today he'd forgotten his first impression of her, standing over him with those forever boots, and she'd just become Shirley. Quirky and courageous and fast with a comeback.

She spun back to him and the dazzling smile died.

'Was she that easy to forget, Hayden?' Hurt blazed in her pale eyes. 'Or was it just some kind of dramatic, absinthe-fuelled gesture for an audience? And you expected everyone else to do the hard yards?'

He *had* pledged. He *had* vowed.

Then he had done nothing. Not one thing.

But he wasn't about to cop to it. 'Why are you so concerned about what I do? How do my choices mean anything at all to you?'

'Because she gave you her life. She gave you all her days teaching and her nights assessing your work and her Saturday afternoons giving her star pupils extra credit.'

'Instead of being with you? Is that what you mean?'

She shook her head. But she also flushed. 'She gave you everything, Hayden. But when she died you just…shrugged and moved on?'

He hadn't worked at the top of his field without learning a thing or two about subtext. This wasn't really about him… He just wasn't sure yet exactly what it was about.

'Every square next to your name is empty. Others have made progress, or at least a start. They've made an effort.'

She was going to ride the denial train right to the end of the line.

'Shouldn't you have let it go by now?' he asked.

She blew air out from between dark lips. 'Yes, I should have.'

The moment of honesty took them both by surprise. She frowned. 'If you told me that you'd been busy building orphanages in Cambodia for the last decade I think I could accept that. But you haven't. You have no excuse.'

He swallowed back what he really wanted to say. 'I don't need an excuse, Shirley. I'm not answerable to you.'

She clutched the towel closer to her pale skin. Her eyes flicked away and back again. 'I just thought you might…'

She didn't want him to do it because she'd make him feel guilty. She wanted him to do it because he was an all-round great guy deep inside. Secretly. 'Hate to disappoint you further, Shirley.'

Her shoulders rose and fell just once as she filled her lungs and moderated her exhalation. Just like her mother used to do before starting a tutorial. Her piled-up hair swung around her face in surf-dampened strands like Medusa's serpentine locks. 'At least take your name off the list. If you're not going to do any.'

So that the world didn't have to look at his disinterest? 'Why don't you add yours? To balance out my lousy effort. Show everyone how it should be done.'

'Maybe I will.' She turned to go, disappointment at his sarcasm patent in the drop of her shoulders.

Honey, I've done a lot worse in my life than let down someone who's been dead for a decade. Your silent judgement can just get in line.

Then she spun back around. 'Molon Labe.'

That threw him. 'What?'

'Your business name. Your tattoo. Why Molon Labe?'

He shrugged. 'Military defiance. When the outnumbered Spartans were called to surrender arms they said Molon labe— "Come and take them".'

'I know. I saw the movie. But *why* that phrase?'

His entire body tightened. 'Because I have a thing for the Spartans. Their courage.' Their defiance in the face of death.

'You don't find the irony exquisite?'

The breath thickened in his lungs. 'What irony?'

'You named your business after it. You branded your body with the Greek letters. Yet, in life, you laid down arms at the first hurdle. You dropped totally off the radar.'

She turned and walked towards the changing rooms. Away from him. Away from the disappointment. Away from the crater her verbal detonation had caused.

He forced his lungs to suck in air and his fingers to open and close again. Forced himself to remember she had absolutely no idea what she was dismissing.

How could she?

But he had enough fight left in him not to let that go unchallenged.

'Shirley,' he called.

She stopped. She turned. She looked ridiculously natural standing there, dripping wet and defiant. But also so very young.

'I understand deflection better than most,' he said without raising his voice across the space between them. Knowing she heard him. 'Attacking me takes the focus off you. But given there's only the two of us here and you clearly don't give a rat's what I think or feel—'

Her extraordinary eyes flickered.

'—you might want to ask yourself what you're trying to take the focus off. And for whose benefit.'

'Cos it sure as hell wasn't his.

Her gaze widened and then dropped to the sand. He turned away from her to climb the dunes up to the road, to find his own way home. He wasn't stupid. No way she was letting him back in her car. No way he'd get in there, even if she did.

Today had been a huge error on his part.

He'd been stupid to think that he could make good on any of his past failings. That just didn't happen.

And something else he knew.

Her stupid purple and black stockings pressing through the beach sand... That was the last of Carol-Anne Marr's crazy, high maintenance daughter that he'd be seeing.

CHAPTER THREE

'You went to Antarctica.'

Not *Hello?* Not *Is Shirley there?* Not *Sorry I was such an exceptional ass*. Shirley took a long slow breath and released it away from the mouthpiece of the phone.

'Hello, Hayden.' She'd know that deep, disparaging voice anywhere.

Instantly.

She'd flown back in yesterday evening and initialled the website just before collapsing exhausted into bed.

Commune with penguins.

Tick.

'That was a big one,' he opened.

'Certainly was,' she closed.

He didn't miss the frost in her tone. 'Listen, about the other day—'

Three months ago.

'—I'd like to apologise.'

Too late. She leaned back in her writing chair. 'No need. I had no right to judge you.'

A long pause from him. Was he trying to decide if she was genuine? 'I could have been more...diplomatic that day. I'm sorry if it hurt you.'

It had hurt but not because he'd slapped her down. Dredging it all up again had hurt. Sifting through her reasons had been hard.

She shrugged. 'The truth does sometimes hurt.'

A long, empty pause. Then, 'I climbed the bridge.'

Shirley's hand froze on the phone. The Sydney Harbour Bridge was on the list. The tiniest of flames puffed into existence deep inside her.

He'd started the list.

'I was there for a stockholder meeting. Thought I might as well.' The flame snuffed out again. Did he add that especially so she'd know how little effort he'd made?

'You didn't tick it off.'

'No, I...' Another pause. But she could hear his breathing. He cleared his throat. 'I thought I'd get a few under my belt before updating the site.'

A few? Did that mean he was going to honour his promise? But she wasn't ready to trust him yet. 'What are you going to do, work your way down the list?'

'The top is as good a place to start as any.'

Sorrow welled up inside, from somewhere deep and dark. 'Well, that should take you about a fortnight, then.'

This time the pause was laden with confusion. His. That was fair enough; she herself barely understood the bitterness creeping through her voice. 'I thought that we could team up for a few of them,' he persevered. 'Two birds, one stone kind of thing.'

Because this was such a massive inconvenience? 'The list is not really a team sport...'

'I enjoyed the dolphins.' A single strand of pleasure twisted through the darkness at his admission. 'The experience I would have had on my own was different to the one I had with you there.'

That was certainly true. 'You would have ended up in a fist-fight with the volunteer.'

'He was smug. And showing off for your benefit.'

'He was passionate. And proud of the work they do. You belittled him.'

'I tested him. Big difference.'

Why did that surprise her? He'd always been interested in breaking people down to see what made them tick. 'Not to the person on the receiving end.'

That shut him up. For almost half a minute.

'So, is that a no to partnering up? I already have reservations.'

She hated doing this by phone. It was all too easy to imagine vulnerability in his tone. If she was looking him in the eye he'd never get away with that. But his tone changed hers. She sighed. 'Tickets to what?'

'The symphony.'

'The Australian Symphony doesn't have Beethoven on their line-up for this year.' She'd already checked.

'Not the ASO. The Berlin Philharmonic. They're in town for a limited season. Three concerts.'

'Those tickets were expensive.' She'd checked that, too.

'So?'

'So throwing money at it is a fast way to get the list out of the way.' And off your conscience.

'Really? I suppose you walked to Antarctica, then?'

'No. I took a work opportunity. There was a media call to promote the hundredth anniversary of the end of Scott's expedition and I qualified. The only thing I paid for was my thermals.'

'Nice junket,' he snorted.

'Sure. If you don't count all the freezing-your-butt-off and hauling yourself up rope nets on and off an ice-breaker.' That had nearly killed her. Although it had helped her get fit preparing for it.

'So how were you planning on getting to Everest without money?'

She tossed back her hair. Maybe it would translate in her voice. 'I don't know. Work on a cruise ship to earn passage. Then make my way to Kathmandu by bike.'

She was nothing if not an idealist.

'It would take a lifetime to do the list that way.'

She stared at the wall. Suddenly something important clicked into place for her. Something she'd been missing.

'"*Full effort is full victory*",' she murmured. Satisfaction lay in the effort, not the attainment. Gandhi knew it. It was just a pity Hayden—the student of human nature—had forgotten what that felt like.

'What?'

She refocused. 'The list was supposed to be about honouring my mother's memory. Buying your way down the list does the opposite.' Almost worse than doing nothing at all.

His pause grew dangerous. 'So, now you *don't* want me doing the list?'

I want you to care. And she had no idea why that was so important to her. 'Not if it means you put in the minimal amount of effort or outsource it to someone to make you up an itinerary.'

Silence descended as he considered that.

'What if I didn't pay for the tickets?'

She blinked. 'Then I assume you'll be arraigned for theft when the curtain rises.'

'Ha ha. I meant that I contra'd them. Does that change how you feel?'

Did it? Last week, if someone had given her a month off work and a cashed-up credit card she would have zoomed through the list knocking things off, too. But she felt sure that there'd be no sense of achievement. Not like the year of preparation for the marathon, or learning to horse-ride well enough to tackle the Snowy Mountains, or working for months on the Antarctica proposal and her ice fitness.

Could she even enjoy the victory if it came so easily?

'Using your influence is like using your money—'

'It wasn't influence. I bartered a friend for the tickets. Good old fashioned labour.'

Labour? Those hands? 'What for?'

'I give you my word it's nothing that wouldn't honour the intent of Carol's list.'

She turned it over in her mind. And over. And then looked under it and really tried very hard to find something reasonable to object to. But her curiosity was piqued, too. What exactly did one trade for tickets to a performance that exclusive?

'Front row?' Okay, now she was just picking a fight.

'Centre.'

'When?' Did he just assume she'd be available?

'Tuesday night.'

Damn. She was.

Somehow it being an evening thing made it feel more like a date than a business arrangement. Which was ridiculous. Two birds, one stone, he'd said. The deal was made. The tickets arranged. Why shouldn't she benefit from whatever hard manual labour he was going to have to undertake to pay them off?

She sighed. 'Okay. I'll see you then.'

'Really?'

Lucky he couldn't see her, because she completely failed to hide the tiny smile that broke at the surprise in his voice. *Too cool for school* was kind of his thing back when she used to watch him from the stairs. It was nice to know that someone who had been that jaded at nineteen was still capable of surprise at thirty.

'Really.'

'Great.' *Awkward.* 'See you Tuesday, then.'

Her chest squeezed tighter at his parting words. But nineteen year old Hayden would never have been a good choice for her and she suspected thirty year old Hayden was even less so.

Lucky this wasn't a date, then.

'Is that a cape?'

Hayden stepped around her in the concert-hall foyer to check out the back of the indigo cloak that Shirley had put on over her simple black dress. The shoulders formed a reverse V that left her décolletage bare and met at an ornate black clasp that closed like fingers around her throat.

'Cape*let,* according to the label,' she informed him.

Whatever it was, it did amazing things to her eyes. And the dress for the rest of her, too.

'You're early,' she announced.

'I wanted to pick up the tickets. You're earlier.'

'I wanted to people-watch.'

At least *Shiloh* did.

He should have twigged when she'd first told him her new name, except that he'd been out of action for so long his connection to the living world had dwindled to what he read in the newspaper and saw on television the few times he turned the thing on.

The fawning of the girl on the beach that day was his biggest clue. That had sent him hunting on the Internet and it took no time at all to realise that *his* Shiloh was *that* Shiloh.

The people's princess.

Blogger extraordinaire.

Queen of snark and acute social awareness.

Possessor of a two-million-plus social network and a list of subscribers that contained every major news journalist, politician's aide and celebrity in the country. No one wanted to be the one *not* following Shiloh's eloquent posts, even if they didn't always like them. Or understand them.

He found the dolphin story—beautifully researched and filled with example after example of people whose lives had been changed following an encounter with a cetacean. Hundreds more in the reader comments. The dolphin that sensed the tumour. Or a pregnancy. A whale that monstered a swarm of sharks away from a flipped catamaran long enough for its passengers to scramble onto the upturned hull. Even a shy manatee that nudged an unconscious boy repeatedly to the surface until help arrived. She'd given the many people who volunteered with wildlife a nod through the voice of that man they'd stood with in the shallows. Yet she'd taken care not to identify the beach location or the animals, protecting them, too.

She knew her boundaries. And her power.

So he'd followed her blogs these past weeks to get a feel for the woman he'd only ever known as a child. She didn't disappoint. Astute. Acerbic. Fearless.

'The symphony's not really the sort of place you'd expect to encounter intriguing story leads.'

'You might be surprised at what people will talk about under cover of a crowd.'

She didn't even blink that he knew who she was. She tossed her hair and a waft of amberwood hit him, provocative and sensual. His breath thinned.

'Are you a regular at the Concert Hall?'

Not really the place he'd bring most of the women he'd dated. 'I've been a few times, but I usually sit up the back.' Right up the back, in the control box with Luc, generally. 'This will be my first front row.'

Her carefully shaped brows folded.

He stepped closer as someone squeezed past them, then looked down on her. 'That surprises you?'

She did her best to step back. 'You don't really strike me as an up the back kind of guy. I thought you'd want to be seen.'

'But you don't know me at all.' Despite what she thought. 'Come on, this way...'

He set off in the direction of the bar, not waiting for her to follow. Ordinarily he'd have found some way by now to touch a woman he'd invited on a date, multiple times if possible while shepherding her through the assembling crowd. But not only was this very much *not* ordinary, and *not* a date and *not* leading to anything further after the instruments were all back in their cases, but he thought Shirley might bite his hand off if he touched her. And he knew for sure she'd object to being corralled like some fragile thing.

She was anything but.

They passed the handful of patrons who'd turned up earlier than they had and crossed to the back area of the bar that served the exclusive members' lounge, past the shelves of expensive drinks. All his old friends lifted their hands in salute, trying to catch his eye. Johnny. Jack. Remy. MacCallan.

He pressed on past them all.

'Luc?'

It took a moment before anyone responded, but then his oldest friend appeared from a pair of doors behind the bar, carrying a sheaf of papers. He clapped forearms with Hayden and did a credible job of not looking at Shirley for more than the time it took to smile politely. Though he knew he'd get hammered for details later.

'Mate, good to see you,' Luc said.

'Is it all arranged?' Hayden asked. Keeping things businesslike.

'Good to go.' Luc reached into his pocket and produced two tickets. He held them aloft. 'These weren't easy to come by. There'll be no reneging?'

Please… 'When have you ever known me not to be as good as my word?'

'I've never asked something like this of you, though.'

Shirley *and* Shiloh both grew interested in that.

He handed over the tickets and Hayden pumped his hand. 'Cheers, mate. I owe you one.'

Luc laughed. 'You know what you owe me.' Then he disappeared back into the bowels of the Concert Hall. Hayden could feel Shirley's gaze branding the back of his head, so he took his time turning around. When he did, her immaculately made-up eyes were narrowed.

'What did you trade?'

He let a cautious nothing wash over his face. 'Oh, just a favour for a mutual friend.'

'What kind of favour? If I'm going to be party to a fraud, I'd like to know exactly what I'm buying into.'

'You're not buying into anything. This was my trade.'

'What was?' Her hands balled on her hips. 'I'm not moving until you tell me the truth.'

Air hissed from between his drawn lips. 'I'm helping out with a party Luc's sister is throwing in a few weeks.'

Her eyes narrowed. 'You mean you're paying for it?'

'No. I told you this wasn't a financial transaction.'

'I didn't realise event coordination was your bag.'

'I'm not organising it, either.'

'Catering?'

He glared at her.

'Not the alcohol, I hope?'

The glare intensified. 'It's not that kind of party. It's for Luc's nephew. He's…' *God damn her snooping.* 'He's nine.'

She blinked at him. A child's party…? Then the tiniest of smiles crept onto her lips. 'Please tell me you're dressing as a clown.'

He threw his arms up and walked across the room from her.

'Do you seriously think that a garden-variety clown would be the best I can do?'

'No, I expect you'd be a miserable, creepy clown.'

He paused, uncertain whether he'd just been insulted. 'Right. Exactly. Thankfully, Tim's not into clowns.'

'What is he into? And why are you trying so very hard not to say?'

He huffed a long breath. 'Warriors.'

Those expressive brows folded again. 'Soldiers?'

He guided her from the bar again without touching her. 'Old school. Swords and shields type of warriors.'

Out of the corner of his vision he saw her press her lips together to stymie the smile he was sure was wanting to burst forth. 'A boy after your own heart, then?'

'That's what Luc said.'

She walked beside him. 'Okay, so for the princely sum of one child's birthday party we now have front row access to the Berlin Philharmonic?'

He shrugged. 'That should give you an idea of how not a big deal this trade is for Luc.'

Her eyes narrowed. 'Or how very big a deal a kid's birthday party is for you.'

He grunted and pushed through the doors back into the foyer, holding it open for her. The noise from the mounting audience surged and washed over them.

'Are you coming or staying?'

It wasn't too late to scalp the tickets out front for a profit.

She let the smile loose, finally. Smug and a little bit too appealing. 'And forgo the chance to make you have to get your Spartacus on?' She pushed past him and spoke into the crowd. 'Not on your life.'

Shirley shuffled in her seat as the applause for the conductor finally died down. She had no idea who he was but every other person there clearly did, judging by the adulation. The white-haired man turned his back on the audience and sorted his music in the descended hush. The perfect acoustics of the venue meant that everyone heard it. Even the shuffling of music sheets sounded good.

Of course, her mother would have chided. *Beethoven wrote it.*

It was hard, as it always was, not to regret her mother's absence. How she would have appreciated this special moment. Then again, if she'd been alive, would any of them have thought of doing it? She'd barely gone to the movies in all of Shirley's childhood, let alone anywhere this special.

That was the awful irony about bucket lists.

'Ready?' Hayden leaned in and whispered. His shoulder brushed hers and the heat pumping off him surged.

The final murmurs from the rows of seating behind and above them stopped and, though nothing in particular was said, the orchestra locked their eyes on the white-haired man in front of them the moment he raised both arms and held them there.

Shirley's breath held, too.

And then they came... The first distinctive notes of Beethoven's Fifth symphony.

Da da da dum...

Da da da dummmmm.

This close, the music was virtually a physical impact. Its volume. Its presence. The hairs curling around her face blew and tickled in the breeze generated only by the synchronised speed of the string section as they commenced their furious playing.

She still hadn't breathed.

Hayden glanced sideways at her as the galloping, excitable violins grew in pitch and strength and she sat up straighter. It wasn't until the trombone had its momentary solo that she heaved in her first breath.

And still he looked.

Amazing, this close, this live. The passion of the performers poured off the stage and washed over her. The drama of the conductor's jerky directions, the rolling synergy of their notes.

Her eyes fell shut.

The music fluttered against her face as it entered the gentle, lyrical interlude which grew and grew.

This was what Beethoven must have experienced when he could no longer hear his music.

And then it came... The discordant counterpoint.

Her eyes opened and she glanced to her right. Hayden was still looking at her. She took a deep breath and returned her full attention to the hammering orchestra. Minutes passed, planets orbited, the poles melted. The music softened for a momentary reprieve. The poignant, forlorn aria of a lone oboe—she wondered how she'd never noticed it before when her mother cranked up her *Best of Beethoven.*

And then the tumbling notes, the controlled descent before returning to the power of the full orchestra for the climax which ended so very like it had begun. Her chest heaved, her heart beat in synch with the strokes of the musical genius. Her body flinched with the explosive closing notes, and she pressed her lips together to stop from crying out.

And then...nothing.

Silence.

The conductor lowered his baton. The orchestra breathed out as one—long, slow and silent.

Shirley turned, breathless, to Hayden. She couldn't clap because no one else was. She couldn't leap up and shout for more, though it seemed ludicrous that music like that wasn't supposed to be celebrated loudly. She could only look at him and hope that her excitement and appreciation were written in her eyes. Her fingers curled around his, hard, as though she could press her thoughts straight through his skin.

His return gaze was complex. Curious. As though she were an alien species he'd just discovered under a rock. But mostly laden with an unexpected quality.

Envy.

Someone behind them coughed. Someone else murmured as the orchestra quietly turned to the next piece. To them this was just another performance. Seven minutes of top-shelf proficiency.

To Shirley it was one of the most extraordinary things she'd ever done.

The audience murmuring grew loud enough that she risked a whisper. But while she might have been able to coordinate her lungs to push air through her voice box, she couldn't quite make the sounds into a meaningful sentence.

'Hayden...' she got out.

He seemed to understand, but his eyes glanced to the stage and then back at her as the conductor called his performers to order with a dramatic flourish and a man she hadn't been aware of stood and walked to a piano she'd barely noticed.

And then it happened...

The first sombre note of the Moonlight Sonata. It wasn't called that on the programme so she was taken unaware. Her eyes were still locked on Hayden's when recognition hit. The music that had played when they'd carried her mother's coffin out of the chapel. The emotional elation of just moments before plunged dramatically as the first haunting notes filled every crevice in the concert hall. She gasped.

Sorrow held her rigid and all she could do was hold Hayden's eyes, his fingers, as the warmth leached slowly from her face.

That horrible, horrible day.

His eyes darkened and his fingers curled around hers in support. She might have cried alone at her mother's funeral ten years ago but this time Hayden Tennant was here with her. Holding on to her. The only other person in the room who knew what this music meant.

Her chest heaves increased as she fought back the tears she could feel forming.

In vain...

Her eyes welled as the beautiful music unfolded in isolation of every other instrument on the stage. The rich, saturated tones of the expensive piano formed a thick private blanket of sound to hide her grief beneath. From everyone but Hayden; he had an unexpected stage-side seat to her pain.

She let her lashes drop to block even him out.

From the sublime to the tragic in the space of two beats of silence. He'd been captivated by Shirley's ecstasy in the face of the music. It had been so long since he'd felt anything, he was quite prepared to feed off her evident joy—her total absorption—like some kind of visceral vampire. He'd been able to stare at her for seven whole minutes unmolested as she reached some place high above the real world.

Buffeted and carried by the music.

Her eyes, when the first famous piece came to a powerful crescendo and she'd gifted him with her focus, had looked as they might in the throes of passion.

Bright, exhilarated, fevered.

And for one breathless heartbeat he'd imagined putting those expressions there, of inciting this strong, unique woman to cast aside the veneer of control that she always wore.

Possession had surged through him, powerful and unfamiliar.

But now those same eyes were off-limits to him, a fat tear squeezing out from under her long dark lashes and rolling down blanched skin. He knew what this music meant and he remembered how Shirley had looked—so small and bereft—the last time he'd heard it.

Her fingers tightened in his as if, by letting go, he'd be casting her adrift on a sea of remembered misery. He curled his other hand over the top and shifted forward so that she might feel his support.

The music turned more melodic, less mournful, and her lids fluttered open to reveal watery, sad eyes, a thousand miles from where they were, lost somewhere in memory. They looked right at him but he knew she wasn't seeing him at all. She was seeing through him.

Exactly as he feared she might if she looked too closely.

That was why she'd never get this close again. After today.

Today she was just a fourteen-year-old girl who needed her mother, and the harder she fought the expression of her feelings, the more he wanted to hold her as she bled her grief out onto the Concert Hall's plush carpet.

He shuffled his arm around behind her and pulled her gently to his shoulder.

The fact she came so very willingly told him a lot about how she was feeling.

They passed the whole piece like that, him curled protectively around her, giving her the privacy she needed, his eyes pressed closed against the evocative music. And against the warmth of the woman in his arms. He felt a few glances from the people around them but he didn't care.

He pressed his lips to her hairline and left them there.

The final notes lingered, eddied around them and then rippled out through the venue and were gone. The audience was completely silent, the hard thrum of blood past his ears the only sound in the place.

The conductor lowered his baton and turned, the pianist stood and bowed, and the audience responded to his cue by bursting into loud fevered applause.

'Shirley…' Hayden said over the din.

Her arm curled around his neck and held him close, her shudder half-swallowed. He gave her a moment, lent her shelter, lent her his strength.

Surprised to discover he had any left at all these days.

But eventually one of them had to move. He cleared his throat. 'Shirley…'

This time she withdrew—in body and in spirit—snaking her arms back into herself and pushing back in her seat. A furious flush stained her pale skin.

'Are you okay—?'

She pushed to her feet, swiping at her eyes. Enough of the audience were on their feet to celebrate the brilliant piano interpretation that their departure wasn't too shocking.

All anyone saw was an overwhelmed woman. They would have no idea what this evening meant to her.

'Are you okay?' he repeated the moment they were in the comparative silence of the empty foyer. A new piece began in the auditorium behind them.

'I'm fine.' She swiped at her eyes with a napkin she'd snatched from a foyer table and kept her eyes off his. 'I just…' She took a deep breath. 'I wasn't ready for it.'

'It's okay to miss her, Shirley.'

Her laugh was harsh. 'It's been ten years. You'd think I'd have a handle on it by now.'

What could he say? 'Would that we could all be loved that much.'

She shuddered in a deep breath and appeared to revive before his eyes. 'Thank you.'

'What for?'

'For arranging this. For her.' She smiled, watery but strengthening, and he realised for the first time how very many smiles she had. And how differently he felt about each one of them.

'I didn't do it for her, Shirley. Or for me.' Her delicate brows flickered. 'I wanted you to have this.'

Not that he had a clue why. It wasn't going to get him anything in return. Nothing she'd give him in a million years, anyway.

Her expression turned awkward. 'You don't think I'd have made it to the symphony unassisted?

'You would have been halfway up the back. You would have heard the music but not...' His fingers grasped for the words he couldn't find.

She lifted her eyes. 'Lived it?'

'Breathed it. She was a wise woman, your mother.'

Shirley sagged. 'I wish I'd known her as an adult, the way you did. To me, she was just my mum. She nagged me about homework and told me to clean my room and what not to wear in public.'

'You took that last one to heart, I see...'

She threw him her fakest smile and he laughed. It felt odd to have run the full gamut of emotions with her in just a quarter of an hour. Exhilaration, devastation and now humour. An intimacy trifecta.

'I would love to have just one adult conversation with her,' she murmured.

He plunged his hands into his pockets to stop himself from touching her. From stroking the sadness from that flawless brow. 'I think she would have been proud of what you do,' he said. 'Of

the way you speak for some parts of the community and challenge others. Of how fearless you are. How provocative.'

She shrugged. 'That's Shiloh.'

He stared at her. 'I'd like to meet Shirley some day.'

Shirley lifted her gaze to Hayden's. 'I don't think she'd be a
match for your sarcasm.'

The tic of his eye was almost a wince. 'But Shiloh is?'

She lifted her chin. 'Shiloh most definitely is.'

They stared each other down as music thumped, muted, from
behind them. Two equals, perfectly matched.

'So the next one is yours,' Hayden finally said.

'Excuse me?'

'Our next adventure. Your choice. Your challenge. See if
you can top this.'

'I didn't realise we were taking turns.' Or doing it again.

'Seems equitable,' he said. 'You're all for equity, I know.'

'You picked a pretty easy one.'

'How about you dress up in a loincloth and brave a house full
of nine year olds, then tell me how easy this one was.'

She stared at him. Thinking. 'All right.'

'All right, what?'

'All right, I'll be your warrior sidekick. For the party. Since I
enjoyed half of the reward today, it seems only fair that I should
pay half the price.'

'You want to come to the kids' party with me?'

Yes. Inexplicably. Maybe it had something to do with seeing how he was with children? You could tell a lot about a man
from how he interacted with animals and kids. Maybe she was
just looking for the kiss of death to her lingering question marks
about Hayden Tennant. To put them to the spear once and for all.

'I'm willing to do my part. In the interests of equity,' she said.

'You'll have to dress up. Or down in this case.'

'Not a problem.'

'You're serious?'

'Completely. Just tell me who you're going as and I'll match
you.'

'You even have to ask?'

'Leonidas.' Of course; the Spartan king who'd first uttered those defiant words. *Come and take them.*

She could well imagine Hayden leading a dwindling army into certain death with defiance on their faces and blood-mingled sweat in their eyes. Barefoot, wild, determined.

Half-naked.

She shifted her eyes away from him as warmth suffused her. Perhaps the party wouldn't be entirely without reward, then. And just like that, she'd decided. Even though saying yes to this was a de facto agreement to undertake more of the list with him.

Her breath thinned. 'When is it?'

'Two weeks Saturday. I'll text you the address.'

She flicked her hair back over her shoulder. 'Great. In the meantime I'll get to work on our next tick off the list.'

How subtly *my* had become *our*. Had she made the mental shift when she'd agreed to come to the symphony with him? Or he'd agreed to go to the dolphins with her? Or was it implicit in the moment she'd curled her fingers so tightly in his during the Moonlight Sonata and she'd not objected when he'd pressed his lips to her forehead?

Maybe he'd branded them *they* with that one gentle action?

Certainly he'd branded her. She could still feel the place his mouth had lingered.

Shirley snorted inwardly. Or was she just a whole lot easier and a whole lot more female than she'd believed? One promise of a bit of gratuitous flesh on show and she totally caved in.

But some concessions were more tingly than others, it seemed. She took a deep breath. Finishing the list was now a combined effort. She had a point to prove about the real meaning of her mother's unfulfilled wish list and she suspected he had his own agenda, his own dark reasons for wanting to prove her wrong.

Yet, somehow, tackling the list with someone else—even if it was a someone else with a vested interest in not succeeding—made it seem less lonely, more achievable. More rewarding.

Even if it was also entirely foolish.

'Okay, see you two weeks Saturday, then.'

He glanced at the large auditorium doors. 'You don't want to go back in?'

Did she? They could walk back in after the first intermission. But how could she top either of those pieces for sheer impact? She looked around for an usher, caught his eye and called him over.

'Hi—' she smiled, one hundred per cent Shiloh '—I've got a sudden migraine and we were front row centre. I'm wondering if you could fill the seats for us? So that the Symphony aren't staring at a hole in their front row?'

The young man smiled. 'Yes, thank you for letting us know.'

He started to move away.

'Actually, do me a favour. Could you find someone way up the back—someone who would die for those seats—and give them to them?'

The man's entire body language changed. 'That's awesome. Yes, I can. I have just the couple in mind. Thank you.'

'You're welcome.' He departed and Shirley turned. Hayden's expression was a mixture of bemusement, curiosity and something else. Something she couldn't quite define. 'What?'

'That was nice.'

'I'm frequently nice; don't look so surprised.'

'No, I mean that was *nice*. I wouldn't have thought to tell them, let alone offer them to someone who was missing out.'

She studied him for a moment. 'I think that says more about you than me, don't you?'

He thought about that. 'Maybe.'

'So... You'll text me?'

'I will.'

'Okay. See you then.' She crossed to the lifts.

'Who will you be coming as?' he called after her. Almost as if he were forestalling her departure.

'I'll let that be a surprise.'

'I hate surprises.'

She turned her head back over her shoulder and gave him

a blast of Shiloh. 'A bit of delayed gratification might be good for you.'

And then she walked out. And left him and his gorgeous suit standing in the foyer all alone.

CHAPTER FOUR

IF HAYDEN'S mouth gaped any further, one of these rampant nine-year-olds was just as likely to mistake it for a bouncy castle and run into it.

'Leonidas—' Shirley bowed '—Boudicca, Warrior Queen of the Iceni.'

She didn't have to worry about how low she bowed; the suspension in the get-up that Andreas had helped her with would have kept Dolly Parton fully immobile. The bodice was more strapping than bra, swathes of earthy fabric wrapped tight around her torso in the manner of the Celts and then flying back over her shoulder to form a cape.

'How did you even get into that thing?' he breathed.

'Andreas helped me.'

'Andreas?'

'My neighbour.'

He quirked an eyebrow, not that she could be certain under his ornate beaten-copper face-shield, which left only his eyes and lips visible, but it tipped slightly and his tone left her in no doubt that it would be lifted beneath the tin.

'Your gay male neighbour?'

Seriously, Hayden? 'My straight seventy-year-old, ex-opera-wardrobe-master-who's-great-with-a-toga neighbour.' The relief on his face was comical. And confusing. 'What does it matter who helped me dress?' she quizzed.

His eyes grew vague. '*Un*dress. Do you think that's appropriate to wear around young boys?'

She glanced down to make sure everything was still where she'd put it. With her long flowing skirts, the only part of her bare was a strip of midriff and her arms and shoulders, which Andreas had carefully decorated with eyeliner tribal tattoos. And her feet, which surely could not offend anyone.

Her laugh was ninety per cent outrage. 'That's rich coming from a man in a miniskirt.'

A thoroughly hot and distracting miniskirt and not a lot else. Leather thong sandals and wrought-copper leg guards protecting his shins—possibly handy if things turned ugly with the nine-year-olds—and some kind of metallic breastplate that accentuated the breadth of his shoulders. Spear with a cork stuck on the dangerous end. Battered shield. And the battle-mask which supported the mother of all mohawks above his head.

That was about it.

Nothing more gratuitous than she'd seen in the water three months ago but somehow infinitely hotter in the suburbs.

What was it about a man in a skirt?

'What did you do to your hair?' he accused.

Had holding that long blunt spear turned him into a caveman? 'I died it. Henna.'

'I liked the black.'

'Strangely enough, your preference didn't really influence my decision. Boudicca had flaming red hair.'

'And she was a brutal warrior. Again, maybe not appropriate for children.'

'Unlike Leonidas, who just carried his spear to pick up litter?'

Luc wandered past them with a steaming bowl of mini red frankfurters in one hand and a family-sized tomato ketchup in the other. 'Come on, you two, the fighting is supposed to be fictional.'

Shirley snapped her mouth shut with a click.

Hayden looked her over once more for good measure, shook his head, then turned and strode away from her. The turning caught his little skirt and gave it extra lift as he marched ahead of her and gave her a better look at his strong thighs.

Would Boudicca have busied herself with the undersides of the Roman tunics? she scolded herself.

A tiny smile crept onto her warrior lips.

I'd like to imagine so.

'You are the best army I've ever led!' Shirley whispered to her seven young boys, hunkered down behind a barrier of rubbish bins and a play house. Every one of them grinned, wide-eyed and excited, through the tomato ketchup now painted on their faces in a replica of her Celtic swirls.

Shirley doled out more fist-sized ammunition.

'I think it's time for a strategy change...' she whispered, laying on a thick accent that was somewhere between Scots and Welsh. And almost certainly nothing like Icenian. 'An army is never as strong without its leader so this time I want you to hurl everything you've got at Leonidas. Take. Him. Out!'

'Yeah!' The boys pumped their fists in the air and took up positions in the cracks between their protective barricade. Across the garden, she could see the erect mohawk of Hayden's Spartan headdress poking up above a hastily constructed shelter made of a deflated paddling pool and some upturned garden chairs and waving as he gave an inspirational battle speech of his own. Then half a dozen little faces peered up over the shelter with their own improvised headdresses on. A cut-down bucket, a foil headpiece, a dustpan brush taped to a head...

It made them easier to find than her stealthy, sauce-smeared Celts.

'Ready...' she whispered, and then surged to her feet, yelling, 'Leonidas!'

'Boudicca!' Across the lawn, Hayden leapt the barrier, thrusting his spear skywards and shouting.

Two mini armies exploded in opposite directions and both let the other pass to run to their real targets. Shirley backed away from the bucket-foil-and-brush-wearing Spartans. As one, they let their missiles fly and she curled her arms up over her head and turned side-on to the assault. Fifteen fat little balloons hit her and burst into a watery mess. High, low, middle. She had to admit, the Spartans were pretty well-coordinated little fighters, whereas her Celts missed more than they hit, then dashed off to pick up the unburst balloons and try again, giggling.

Hayden made much of his watery death, eventually falling flat in a blaze of glory on the suburban lawn. The Celts piled on, cheering. Then the Spartans piled on top.

'Okay, warriors...' Tim's mum intervened loudly, plucking the first of the children off a beleaguered Hayden. 'You have restored peace to this land and now a mighty feast awaits the victors in the kitchen.'

The boys and their bottomless energy fled into the house on a chorus of cheers.

Shirley plucked at her saturated bindings and dragged the wet fabric away from her legs. Her hair and the beaded Celtic inserts she'd woven in dripped more water onto her.

Hayden sauntered towards her, grinning. 'Quite the battle.'

Her pulse sky-rocketed. 'You were annihilated; dead men can't speak,' she puffed.

'You took a few mortal wounds yourself, judging by all that blood.'

It wasn't red but it dripped off her like the real thing. It dawned on her then that she hadn't really thought through the rest of this day. Or brought a fresh change of clothes. She'd imagined she'd be getting back into her car in the same state she'd got out of it.

Spot the one with no experience with children!

'They're amazing. So much energy.' She peeled her skirt from her thighs again but it returned, limpet-like, and so she gave up. 'I need a rest.'

She crossed to the Spartan camp and flipped both chairs upright and then dragged one into the sun. Half-in, half-out. Hayden flopped down next to her and thrust a tube of wet wipes at her.

'Here... Your face seems to have worn most of the carnage.'

Given how heavily tattooed it was with eyeliner, that didn't surprise her. She pulled a couple of the wet wipes out and set to work erasing the evidence of her slaughter, while the rest of her body slow-dried in the afternoon sun. But wiping off the Celtic make-up also took her regular make-up with it.

Still, no real choice unless she wanted to sit here looking shambolic.

Hayden lay stretched out on his lawn chair in his full Spartan glory, practically glistening from the paraffin added to the water balloons to stop them from popping too easily. Shirley stole a couple of peeks as she methodically removed every trace of make-up from her face.

'Leonidas suits you,' she said absently. Golden. Lean. Strong. Not bad for a hermit. Or a CEO.

He tipped his head sideways. 'I have to admit feeling very much like I could have been in his army a hundred lifetimes ago.' He didn't go back to studying the sky. 'You missed a bit.'

He tapped his nose but that wasn't terribly helpful without a mirror.

'Here...' He swung his legs over the edge of the lawn chair, plucked a fresh wipe from the container and slid his sunglasses up onto his head. 'Sit still.'

The move brought him closer than he'd ever been. Breath-stealingly close. He methodically removed the last of her make-up, gently turning her face side to side to make sure he missed none. When he was done, his eyes came back to hers. Her chest squeezed.

'And there she is...' he murmured, a half-smile twisting his lips. 'Nice to finally meet you, Shirley.'

The intensity of his gaze was infectious. Her breath struggled for function. 'We've met, actually.'

The smile grew. 'Not like this. Not formally.'

'You don't remember?'

He lowered his fingers, frowned. 'At the funeral?'

She shook her head. 'Before that. Long before that.'

He stared, his busy mind working furiously. 'I don't remember. I'm sorry.'

No. 'I wouldn't expect you to. It was nothing, from your point of view.'

But it had changed her life. She'd hit puberty on the spot. At eleven.

He sat back but didn't lie down again. He held her trapped in his gaze. Silence fell between them.

'Seriously, how long before your black hair comes back?' he blurted.

She laughed. 'For a man who's only ever been photographed with blondes, you certainly have a fixation with my hair colour.'

'I don't hate the red but I really liked the black.'

That brought a very different colour to her cheeks and she knew that he'd clearly see it, sans make-up. 'Actually it's called "Raven". The colour.'

He laughed. 'Of course it is. Very Edgar Allan Poe.'

Luc emerged with two tall glasses of iced water and he passed them one each. 'You guys should hire yourselves out as a double act,' he said. 'That was awesome.' Then he reached out and passed something else to Shirley. 'I got these from your bag for you, I hope you don't mind. It's bright out here.'

Sunglasses! As good as a face full of make-up when they were the size hers were. She slid them on. It was like sliding a mask back into place.

'Thank you, Luc. And thanks again for the other week at the Concert Hall; it was so wonderful.'

His eyes dragged quickly over Shirley's still drying, still snug form. She felt much more exposed when Luc looked at her than when Hayden had, but when Hayden looked she felt *naked*. In a good way. A dangerously good way.

Hayden glared pointedly at his friend.

'No problem,' Luc said, oblivious. 'You more than paid it off today.'

'I told you, it's going to be hard to top,' Hayden joked. 'You haven't forgotten that the next one is yours, have you, Shirley?'

She turned her focus more fully back to him, sitting perched on the chair still facing her. Seriously, had a man ever looked more ridiculous or more comfortable in a short skirt? Or more gorgeous?

'Not only have I not forgotten, but it's all arranged. I was going to tell you about it today.'

His eyes grew keen. Warmed with challenge. 'How? You've either done everything else already or it's overseas…'

She stared at him.

He frowned. 'We're going overseas? On no money?'

'Okay, this one is on *some* money, but not much. About one hundred dollars each way.'

His eyebrows lifted.

'And…' she said, readying to deliver her *coup de grâce* '…we get to tick off two things from the list.'

'For one hundred dollars?' Disbelief saturated his voice.

She smiled and turned her un-made-up face to the sun for some rare vitamin D. 'You'll just have to trust me.'

'Dangerous words, bro,' Luc said, standing, and looking at Hayden. 'Now, you need to throw some clothes on before all the mums start arriving and drive through my sister's hedges in distraction,' he said with a smile, then turned to her, 'and you need to cover up before Hayden tips right off that lawn chair. I have the important job of distributing the party bags.'

She glanced at Hayden, who busied himself studying the underside of the eaves.

Luc sauntered back into the house and an awkward silence fell. Until that moment she'd really not been all that bothered by the suction of her clothes to her curves, but it bothered her now. Luc's suggestion bothered her.

As in hot and bothered.

She stared at the *MΩΛΩN ΛABE* tattoo on his shoulder. Shoulder seemed suitably modest.

'I think you should stay as you are,' she joked. 'And go out onto the street to welcome the mums.'

Even white, teeth sparkled. 'You're evil.'

'I'm a student of human nature. Isn't that what you once said?'

'Luc's right; I need to cover up.' He pushed to his feet and peered down at her. She lifted her hand to screen the bright sun.

He was gloriously broad in silhouette but it meant she couldn't see his face.

'And he's right about why you need to cover up, too.'

'So what's her story?' Luc said from behind him as Shirley's purple monstrosity drove away. With a still dripping Boudicca in it.

'No idea,' he murmured, still following her departure until she turned the corner. Then he dragged his eyes back to his friend. 'She's just a girl. The daughter of one of my lecturers.'

Luc laughed. 'She's not *just* an anything.'

He turned back to the empty road where her car had just been. *No.* Not even close.

'I assume you know what you're doing?' Luc went on as he thrust two party bags in the hands of the last departing nine-year-olds.

Hayden looked up. 'Meaning?'

'First the symphony, now Tim's party? That's not your usual playbook. And she's a total deviation from your usual type. I assume you're working an angle?'

Really? That was Luc's first assumption when his mate brought a nice girl over. Not that he didn't deserve the suspicion. 'No angle. I'm helping her with something.'

'Yeah, you're a regular Sir Galahad,' Luc snorted. 'You're hot for her. It's obvious.'

'That's not why I'm helping her...' Not that there wasn't a lot to be hot about. 'It's just a chance to get to know her.' That generated a modicum of stunned silence from his usually unflappable mate. Hayden turned. 'What?'

Luc masked his surprise. 'Nothing. Just never thought we'd have this moment.'

'Me standing in a skirt on your sister's verge?' No doubt.

Luc wasn't deterred. 'You admitting to interest in a woman.'

'I've had a lot of female interests. Far more than you, mate.'

Luc wasn't biting, either. 'Not like this, Hayds. Not someone normal.'

A laugh shot out of him. 'Shirley is far from normal.'

'You're doing stuff together, getting to know her, flirting...'

He turned for the house. 'That wasn't flirting. I was just entertaining myself.'

'Please. It was practically foreplay. If you're just amusing yourself then you might want to think about what that will do to her. She's not in the same league as the other women you've dated.'

Luc's words produced a fiery, blazing desire to be sure Shirley wasn't tarred by the brush of the many women he'd been with. Which in turn produced the confusing question—*why?* So of course he said the exact opposite of what he thought. 'She seemed up for it. She's stronger than she looks.'

'Steel's strong, too, until the moment it's not.'

Time for a new conversation. He swished back towards the house, Luc in tow. 'It's not going to be an issue. She's far too switched on to have a bar of me.'

'You might surprise yourself, Hayden. If you let someone in, they might want to stay.'

A dark, thick pool deep inside burped up a puff of uneasiness like a boiling tar pit. 'Maybe I should leave you my skirt, mate. If you're going to get all huggy on me.' He snagged up his sports bag full of street clothes. 'I do this for a living, Luc. For entire corporations. I think I can read one twenty-four-year-old woman, don't you?'

'I'm not worried about whether you can read *her,* Hayds,' he said. 'I'm worried that you don't read *you* all that well sometimes.'

Yeah, he did; better than his friend thought. Well enough to recognise when he had no idea what he was doing. Yet. But being in the dark wasn't the same thing as being oblivious. Leonidas would have agreed. Even if you didn't know exactly how many were in the opposing force or what weapons they were carrying, just knowing they were over the horizon was a huge advantage.

Forewarned was forearmed.

CHAPTER FIVE

'YOU realise the next time you say "Trust me, Hayden" I'll just laugh and remind you of this moment.'

They stood, suitcases in hand, on the dock of the port. The wrong side of the dock. The bright white, multi-storey cruise liners all lined up on the far side. On this side the dirty barnacle-encrusted freight liners slummed it.

Hayden stared at the hulking great vessel in front of them, with its towering patchwork of sea-containers. 'When you said pack for a sea voyage I had something very different in mind.'

Beside him, Shirley smiled. 'What did you expect for a hundred bucks each way?'

He sighed and closed his eyes. What had he expected? He'd had vague dreams of crewing on a maxi-yacht, or working for their passage on one of the leisure behemoths on the far side of the port. 'Not this.'

'I have a friend at the port authority. She gave me the tip about this vessel. It comes in fully laden and then offloads half its cargo and crew for shore leave before heading on to New Zealand to drop the rest and return half-full. Then they pick up their shore-rested crew and new cargo.'

She was staring at him with such enthusiastic expectation. He just kept staring at the vessel.

'So they have room for passengers there and back,' she went on. 'The catch is that you only get one day in New Zealand. But that's all we'll need.'

He nodded slowly. How else were they going to get to New

Zealand for the bungee jumping or Venice for the gondola ride, or the base camp of Everest? The list wouldn't have been easily achievable even for her mother. Some parts of it they had no hope of delivering.

This was pretty clever. But he wasn't about to give her that just yet.

'I hope they're not expecting me to haul containers?'

She nudged him bodily. 'Come on, Leonidas, I've seen your muscles.'

And that was all it took. An unexpected bit of full body contact and he was totally on board with this crazy plan. He stared at the *Delphi Paxos* and worked hard to ignore the tingling place in his arm where the curve of her breast had just brushed. 'As long as I can get a satellite signal then I can keep the shareholders happy for the week I'll be away.'

She glanced up at him. 'I know it's not the Ritz—'

Oh, honey, it's not even The Ritz's off-site warehouse.

'—but it's a virtually free ride to New Zealand and it puts two ticks in boxes.'

Ticks in boxes. Right. Everything was about the boxes with her. How had he forgotten?

She set off across the dock tarmac, pausing to let a kamikaze forklift whizz by. They reached the bottom of a long skinny gangplank. Shirley ground to a halt just in front of him. He peered around her to check her expression.

'I just...um...' she muttered.

He stepped around her and looked at her front-on. 'You okay?'

She took a deep breath. 'It's stupid...'

This whole thing was stupid but it meant something to her so here they were. 'What is?'

'I've never been on a boat. It looks so much bigger from here.'

Uh-oh. 'Never?'

She shook her head. 'Only river ferries.'

'Well, that's exciting then.' God loved an optimist. Yet the hint of vulnerability certainly wasn't *un*appealing.

She chewed her lip and raised her eyes up the side of the enormous hull. 'I hope so.'

'Once you're up there it won't look so big. I promise.'

But he couldn't promise what a novice would make of the pitch and roll of the Tasman Sea. Her clever solution wasn't going to look too great when she was face down over a toilet bowl for four days. Or the bow of the ship.

He took her hand and drew her upwards. Took a step. Then another. She followed him up the long skinny gangplank. They were met at the top by a smiling man who greeted them in heavily accented English.

'Welcome to ship!'

He glanced around at the heavy fittings, the utilitarian paint job. Yup, definitely a working vessel. But it did at least look solid. And clean. And much less daunting from on deck for his suddenly nervous novice.

Their crew member told them in broken English that Immigration would come through before the ship was cleared for departure and to have their passports ready, and to stay in their cabin until they'd been cleared.

Amongst so many mispronunciations, that little one slipped him right by.

At least until the man flung a small door wide and cheerfully announced, 'Room!'

The cabin was tiny but it had two neat beds in it. Skinny single beds. Shirley looked at the seaman sideways. 'Whose room?'

'Yes. Your room.'

'But which? Mine or his?'

The lines on his weathered face multiplied. Shirley grew dangerously still and the man started babbling in his own tongue. It was Greek. Greatly evolved from the ancient Greek Hayden had studied during his classical units, but close enough.

He stepped in and fumbled his way to offering to help in classical Greek. The man instantly refocused on the closest approximation to his own language in the room.

'How many cabins did you book?' he said quickly to Shirley.

'Two. Of course, two.' Furious colour crept ever higher.

He did his best to communicate the dilemma. The crewman nodded and shot back in rapid-fire Greek.

'I think he's agreeing with you.' The man held up two fingers. 'Two.'

'Damn right he is...' Shirley started to fan her hot face with her passport.

The crewman picked up Hayden's suitcase and placed it on the foot of the bed and then he picked up Shirley's and walked out of the room with it, crossed the tiny hallway and opened a door there to a room the twin of the first. He dumped her suitcase on the end of a bed in there. And then turned to check her understanding. Baffled but optimistic.

'Okay...?'

'Okay,' she said through a tight smile.

On the bright side, the distraction seemed to have made her forget all about her sea nerves.

She moved into her cabin.

'There are worse things in this life than sharing a room with me,' he joked. 'Women have cage-fought for less.'

She threw him her most withering glare. He loved that one.

'Seriously,' he probed carefully. 'Why are you so angry?'

She pressed her lips together. 'Because it was shaping up to be a stupid situation and I'm not accustomed to doing stupid things.'

He snorted. 'By contrast, I'm delighted to discover that you're fallible.' Way too pleased to be bothered at the thought of sharing a room. In fact, one tiny part of him was disappointed. The part that liked her best off-kilter.

She frowned at him. 'I didn't want you to think... It looked like...'

She fanned more furiously.

Oh... She didn't want him to think she'd planned it that way. Accidentally on purpose. 'You know you don't have to come up with convoluted excuses to sleep with me, Shirley. I'm easy. Or haven't you read the papers?'

She had roughly the same number of glares as smiles and he enjoyed them just as much.

'Easy? Hardly.'

But she kept her distance, he noticed. He flopped down on one of the tiny beds.

Her startled face returned to him. 'What are you doing?'

'Waiting for Immigration. We might as well save them some time and wait together.'

She grunted and set about transferring the contents of her suitcase into the stand-up locker in the austere room. He watched her crossing back and forth across the tiny space. Her movements were fluid, graceful. More dancing than walking. The items she was unpacking were mostly dark and plain. Not at all what he'd become used to her wearing.

'What?' she challenged on her third pass.

'I was expecting something more…nautical.' And how strange that he felt genuine disappointment at its absence. He'd grown used to her particular brand of fashion.

She straightened and turned. Considered him. 'Not really practical at sea. Most of what I've brought is supremely suburban.'

He stared at her. 'Does that mean no make-up?'

'*Pfff.* Don't be ridiculous.'

He tucked his hands behind his head. 'What if I challenged you?'

She frowned. 'To what?'

'You challenged me to do the list on a budget. What if I challenge you to do it in civvies with no make-up?'

'Why would you?'

He couldn't think of a clever answer to that so he went for honest. 'Because I got such a short glimpse of Shirley at Tim's party. And because that way we're both out of our comfort zones.'

And because I'm dying to know what colour your lips really are. He stared at them now, stained with dark lipstick, and imagined wiping it off with his thumb.

She stared him down. Thinking. 'All right.'

He knew her too well to imagine she'd just capitulate. All they'd done since meeting was trade—insults, tasks, looks— this wasn't going to be any different. 'But…?'

'I'll ease up on the make-up while we're on this trip if you'll answer a question. Honestly.'

The keen glint of her eye should have been warning enough. But he was too dazzled by it to recognise it straight away. 'Okay.'

'What was your fascination with my mother?'

His gut tightened up immediately, the bad old days still not his favourite pre-dinner conversation. But he'd agreed to be honest. 'She was a great teacher.'

Those eyes so very like her mother's narrowed. 'Every Saturday for three years?'

He stood. This conversation just didn't feel right with him stretched out on the tiny bed. Shirley crossed her arms, taking the leggings she was still holding with her. They bunched across her torso.

'She knew so much. She gave us one hundred per cent of her focus.' Which was a bit rough when that left nothing for her daughter, he suddenly realised. But at the time he'd simply craved a motherly connection. Anyone's mother would have done.

'I didn't have...access to my own mother. Spending time with yours was good for me. She helped keep me grounded. Her expectations. She set a high bar.'

'Tell me about it,' Shirley muttered, then cleared her throat and said, louder, 'You were pretty cut up when she died.'

He had been. Everything he'd shoved way down deep to survive his mother's death had come bubbling back up at Carol's. Except he had found something to console him, eventually. A series of somethings: pills, women, alcohol, in that order. And they'd got him through that loss and out the other side. And then they'd propped him up well into the next decade. Until he'd gone cold turkey on all three a few years ago.

Saved his life.

'Nothing compared to your loss, I imagine,' he murmured.

She shut that line of conversation down with the not very subtle zip of her empty suitcase. 'I always wondered where you'd gone for your knowledge fix after that.'

'I didn't. It was never about the knowledge for me.' It was about having a mother figure in his empty life.

She glanced back up at him. 'Then why do it?'

He shrugged. 'I was good at it.'

She turned back. 'I'm sure you were good at a lot of things.'

Not if you'd asked his father. Or his other lecturers. 'Really? What else? Cutting up the athletics track? Musical accomplishment? Do you think a masterful maths mind lurks in here?' He tapped his forehead.

'Masterful enough to run a successful business. Even more successful recently.'

He stared at her, a warm realisation leaching through his body. She'd been checking up on him. 'Someone else has been busy on Google, then.'

She stiffened, but ignored him. 'I thought you walked away from your business for a reason.'

Her green eyes bored into him, towards the truth that lurked deep within. 'I realised it was easier to change the business than myself.' And who he'd become was so tightly enmeshed with what he did. He'd needed some healthy distance in order to untangle it all.

'Changed it to what? From what? It's so hard to tell from your website.'

Why not? She'd find out eventually. It might as well come from him. 'I did my Masters in Influence.'

Her snort was the least ladylike and most sexy he'd ever heard. This woman just didn't care for the slightest pretension. 'Did you make that up?'

'No. It's made me rich.'

'You have some massive clients. That much I could tell.'

'Clients who paid generously for a look into the hearts and minds of their future customers.' She frowned and her eyes grew keen, and he remembered who he was also talking to: Shiloh. But—inexplicably—he also trusted her. 'Their businesses revolve around knowing where to target likely customers and what will get their buy-in.'

She stared at him. 'That's...'

'The word you're looking for is "lucrative".' It wasn't, but it was true.

'Which doesn't make it any more palatable.'

He tipped his head and granted her that. It was no more than he'd eventually come to think. The day he'd realised how closely all those 'somethings' that he consoled himself with were linked to his profession.

'Show me.'

He looked up. 'Show you what?'

'How it works. On me.'

'Oh Shirley, I don't think you're the same as everyone else. I wouldn't begin to claim I understand how your mind works.' Disappointment stained her already dark lips. He thought fast. 'But I can show you how you did it to me.'

Show her how it was inherent in everyone—even the virtuous Shiloh. Bred into the human species.

She sat on the edge of the second bed and folded her hands on her lap. It was entirely demure and insanely provocative.

'Influence is all about buy-in,' he started. 'Once you can get someone to say yes to something small they make a mental commitment to that thing and transitioning them to something bigger is more straightforward. If I want you to buy my car I get you to sit in it. If I want you to borrow money from me as an adult I give you a money box when you're a child. If I want you to accept my faith I get you to accept something smaller from me first.'

Her eyes slowly rounded as he spoke.

She might as well know who she was dealing with. 'You wanted me to do the list. You got me to let you into my house first.'

'Actually, I let myself in.'

'But I didn't throw you out. In the exact moment I accepted your intrusion, I bought-into your quest. I gave you something small—my attention—then you incrementally asked for more.' His eyes fell to her lips, which had parted softly. 'A few hours of my time to do the dolphins. Then a commitment to spend a lot more of my time working out how to do it on the cheap. Then you triggered my natural competitiveness and got me to buy in even further. And now we're sitting on a freighter getting ready to go to another country.'

'All because you let me into your house?' she breathed.

'All because you got me to commit a tiny part of myself to this quest. And the moment I made the mental shift there was no turning back.'

'I didn't mean to do any of that.' Heat rushed up her cheeks.

'Yes, you did, you just didn't name it. No one does.' He shrugged. 'I've made my business out of naming it.'

Out of selling his soul. For top dollar.

She watched him steadily. Read him correctly. 'So why do you still do it?'

The million-dollar question. The answer would be worth that if anyone could give it to him.

'Because I can?'

'Is that a good enough reason?' she murmured. 'Just because you can?'

'And because someone else would if not me.'

'Why don't you just leave them to it?'

'Because they won't do it as well as me.' He'd chosen that profession and he was good at it. The best. It was about the only validation he got these days.

Her curious green eyes dug deep. Trying to figure him out. There was more he could say, things that would only add to her confusion. But he didn't because they would only smack of justification.

'Anyway. That's how it's done. In life. In love. In everything.'

'Not love—surely?'

'Love isn't special. Or different. You just have to find the in-point. Something small.'

'That makes it sound very calculated.'

He shrugged. 'What is seduction if not entirely calculated?'

'We were talking about love, not seduction.'

'What's the difference?' Then it hit him. 'You don't believe that love is something that just happens without effort?'

She frowned and colour pricked at her cheeks.

'How can Shiloh operate on the sharp edge of the sword when it comes to every other aspect of contemporary life, yet still buy into the whole romantic love myth?'

'You don't believe in falling in love?' she bristled.

'That implies some kind of uncontrolled accident of fate. Love is a steady, intentional climb towards a goal.'

'You speak from experience?'

'I speak from centuries of experience.' Other people's experience. Myriad lives across time.

She lifted one brow. 'And the centuries tell you that seduction and love are the same thing?'

'They're symbiotic. Seduction is the best part of love.'

'Spoken like a true man,' she grunted. 'Somehow, I thought you'd be a devotee of the meeting of intellects being the purest form of love.'

He looked down on her. 'You think Plato or Socrates didn't consider mental sparring as a kind of seduction?' She wanted to deny it—he could see it in her troubled expression.

'Surely there has to be a physical attraction?' she pressed.

'It's a bonus but not essential.'

Keen green eyes fixed on him and he could see her sharp brain taking hold exactly as it had at the dolphins. Her mind was engaged. Great, he could work with minds.

'So how would you start a seduction of a complete stranger?' she asked. 'If I brought the question to Molon Labe as a business hurdle?'

He folded his arms and pretended to consider it. He didn't need to. This stuff came so naturally to him after all this time. In fact, even before that, human nature had always been so very obvious to him. The links between people, their motivations and drivers. It had taken him years to realise the rest of the world was more or less oblivious to that.

'You have to start with the ultimate goal. Do you want to feel desired? Get married? Be loved?' He locked his eyes on hers. 'Or do you just want to scratch that itch that burns like fire-ants under your skin?'

She swallowed hard, but her pupils grew bigger. 'Let's keep this tasteful. Let's say married.'

So Shirley Marr blushed like a schoolgirl at the thought of

sharing a room with him and wanted to be desired and loved but wasn't saying so.

Interesting.

He thought about it for a few moments, for effect. 'Marriage is a commitment. So your first step is to find a way to get a man to commit to the idea of commitment itself.'

'How?'

He searched the air for ideas. A hundred came to him immediately. 'Start a project together. Travel. Buy a puppy. Put a vegetable patch in. Get him to give you a space for your toothbrush at his place. Anything that requires him to lock a part of himself into something.'

The dark hair mounded on her head tipped as she considered that.

'Once he's made the mental shift towards commitment, then it's just a series of incremental rises until he's totally on-board with the idea of a permanent commitment.'

She stared at him. 'No wonder you're so cynical. If that's what you believe people do.'

'I'm not saying it's conscious, necessarily.'

'Surely being aware of it means it wouldn't work?'

He laughed. 'You wanted me to commit to the list and I did. Knowing what was happening didn't stop it from working.'

She chewed her lip. Suddenly two hundred per cent of his focus centred there.

'A demonstration, perhaps?' he murmured.

Her eyes darkened and widened within their kohl smudges as she stared up at him warily.

'I find myself very interested in the shape and taste of your lips,' he said theatrically. 'And I'm declaring that to you so you're aware of the direction of my thoughts and so you can plan to resist when the moment comes.'

And because success will be so much more satisfying that way.

He reached down and pulled her to her feet. She rose to stand before him.

Shirley had to push extra-hard to get words past her suddenly tight chest. 'This is hypothetical, I assume?' Hayden's smile reminded her of the Huntsman-wolf in Red Riding Hood. *All the better to eat you with...*

'If that makes you feel better about your chances of resisting,' he said.

He pulled her a little closer. Closed his arms around her, hot and strong. Her heart went berserk. 'So the question is, Shirley...knowing what I'm doing and knowing what my goal is—' he breathed down on her '—are you any less inclined to let me kiss you?'

She licked her lips. Struggled for air. 'You're assuming you already have my buy-in?'

Hayden blinked, slow, confident. That caused Shirley's own lids to follow suit, growing heavier. She tried to glance away to break the contact.

'A kiss is the touching of flesh on flesh. You started to buy into me touching you months ago...the first time you let my glance rest on your porcelain skin. Then later, when you let my fingers graze your hair. Then take your hand. Even now...my eyes are roaming where my lips cannot and you're allowing it.'

Sure enough, his veiled gaze browsed her mouth and made it part in breathless anticipation. She forced it closed.

'And now, even knowing what I plan to do and why, you're still in my arms. I think I'd call that buy-in.'

'Pretty clever,' she breathed, desperate to preserve some dignity. 'Assuming it's going to be any kind of kiss at all.'

His teeth flashed white and dangerous. 'And there it is. Full commitment.'

He took her weight on his arm and leaned her back into it, his mouth pressing down confidently onto hers, sliding against it, still half-smiling in his victory. She held firm against the heavenly feel and smell of him so close, refusing to give in.

She would have loved to stand, unmoved, in his hold. To let him kiss her senseless and then to emerge untouched. Indifferent.

But that wasn't going to happen.

Not in this lifetime.

The moment she resisted, holding her own—barely—against the breathless spin of her mind, he upped the ante. Plying her with the technique that must have unzipped many a skirt in its time. His mouth glided over hers, alternating pressure, his tongue teasing the firm line she maintained where her lips met. His flesh blazing against hers. Her head spun wildly.

He pulled back a little, breathed words against her flaming skin, and something about the shift of colour in his eyes told her he wasn't playing a game any more. 'I'm going to kiss that dark gloss off until I reveal what's underneath it.'

A sudden erotic lance speared way down deep inside. He set to work doing just that, pressing himself more fully into her, binding them close and kissing the living daylights out of her. Her fingers, pressed against his chest to stop him getting closer, curled, of their own accord, into the fabric of his shirt. Her feet, which she'd positioned to help her push against Hayden, subtly shifted weight so that she leaned more fully into him.

Into his kiss.

Her head, which should have been screaming resistance, swam uselessly in the wash of scent and sensation pumping off the human hormone holding her up.

And her mouth opened.

Instantly he was in, his triumph punctuated by the thrusts of his tongue and the heaving breaths they both stole between kisses. Her whole body flamed with desire and she speared her fingers up into his hair, keeping him close. He backed her up against the wall.

'Witch,' he pressed into her hungry lips. 'There was never any other avenue for us.'

Something about speech. Something about the incendiary way the two of them had burst to flame the moment they touched and the way the oxygen they sucked in only fuelled it more. *Something* finally drew her attention to what they were doing and where.

She pulled back, chest heaving. 'You assume that was all your doing,' she whispered the moment her lips were free. 'What if I've been angling for a kiss since the beginning?'

His eyes darkened, dropped. Then his hands followed suit. Then he stepped away.

'That's the other key principle of influence,' he heaved, dragging his wrist across his lips. 'Convincing the subject it was their idea all along.'

And then he was gone, back across the hall to his own room, leaving her half sagging against the cold steel wall of the cabin.

Damn you, Hayden Tennant.

It was minutes before she had the strength to lever herself upright away from the wall long enough to sag down onto the little bed.

Had she ever before wanted something as badly and resented it so thoroughly as that kiss? She hated the fact that she was no more a match for his seduction than any of the other women he'd targeted and overpowered. And she *really* hated the fact that he'd been so supremely confident of her capitulation. Was he that sure of his own prowess or did he think her so lacking in resolve and character?

Quite accurately, as it turned out. On all fronts.

Should she cut herself some slack that it was—without question—the best kiss she'd ever received? That it jammed electrodes into parts of her that usually slumbered happily and forced them into sparking, buzzing animation until they lurched to life like the Frankenstein of body organs. It was as surreal and un-forgettable—and futile—as being snogged by some handsome movie star who kissed for a living. What hope did she have?

Yeah, that was satisfactory. No personal responsibility required at all, then.

'Ugh.' She bounced her head a few times on the neat pillow in its faintly diesel-smelling coverslip.

Of course she was responsible.

She'd been on slow simmer since the day of Tim's party, having filled her imagination and the weeks since with images of an oil-slicked, half-naked Hayden sprawled so comfortably on that lawn chair. Yet strangely, it had been his comfort—not his state of undress—that had particularly appealed to her that day. She'd stretched out alongside him, dripping and smiling, and felt such an astonishing sense of amity for the man she'd only sparred with until then. Fellowship made a nice change from the thin edge of conflict or the dangerous high-wire of attraction. The best parts of being with Hayden were just...being.

But she knew which part got her pulse racing hardest.

She lifted her fingers to her lips.

So he'd kissed her. So what? He was just making a point. It just happened that he was as good a point-maker now as he had been when he was younger. Thorough and convincing. And she'd been well convinced by his kiss.

Right up until the moment he'd taunted her that it was fake and walked out of the room.

She rubbed the puffy skin of her bottom lip. Ridiculous. It was *not* still tingling. It was projection. It had just been a really spectacular kiss from someone self-proclaimed in the art of seduction. And she was generally hormone-deficient, so hitting a charisma bomb like Hayden was bound to have an impact.

Not *deficient;* that was hardly fair to a body that was capable—more than capable, apparently—of simmering. Perhaps *suppressed* was a better word. If you denied something long enough, your body eventually stopped expecting it.

Shirley blew air slowly out through still-pulsing lips.

She needed fresh air. Perspective.

She needed to get away from his lingering scent and the breath-stealing memory of him bending her back in his arms and plundering her mouth. Like the pirate he was. The stealer of kisses. And of dignity.

Half an hour in the bracing air of the Tasman Sea would do her wonders.

It might even help distract her from the all-encompassing desire to find Hayden and to pick a fight with him again, just to keep her arousal levels up. Up where he'd left them dangling so helplessly. So wasted.

If she couldn't kiss him, she could shout at him a little bit and release tension that way.

CHAPTER SIX

HE'D made his point but he didn't feel particularly good about it. Hours later and far out to sea, Hayden was still rattled by that kiss. The kiss he'd initiated then rapidly lost control of.

He'd lost control before, but it was always a carefully reined surrender. Even letting himself go came with some strict rules and recovery solutions. At all times.

With Shirley he'd literally lost it. His body participated in direct defiance of his will. On its own agenda. Nice little karmic reward for being a bastard and bending her to his will.

Just because you can...

He released his fingers from the punishing fists he'd made standing there at the bow of the *Paxos,* resting his arms on the aperture in the high wall which protected the crew and cargo from potentially high seas. Other people clenched their teeth when they were stressed, he clenched his fingers. To the point of pain.

It was unconscious but it made his dentist happy.

'Hayden.'

Shirley spoke, soft and tentative, behind him. Knowing he was the cause of her uncertainty only infuriated him more. He turned slowly and faced the music.

She was in black from head to toe but it was just a T-shirt and leggings and she'd toned her make-up right back to a translucent foundation. Closer to what it had looked like the day she'd wiped Boudicca from her skin. Hayden stared at her and she shifted uncomfortably under his scrutiny. When he wasn't being distracted by dramatically highlighted eyes and burnished coffee lips it was possible to appreciate the fine texture of her skin. He'd attributed its smoothness to her make-up. But it looked as if it was all natural.

He cleared his throat. 'You honoured our bargain.'

One elegantly plucked brow arched. 'You thought I wouldn't?'

'I thought I might have voided it.' *By kissing you.*

She glanced away briefly. 'I asked you a question and you answered it. It wouldn't be reasonable to protest.'

'Most people would.'

'I'm not most people.'

No. She wasn't.

'Anyway, I came to get you. There's something you need to see.'

'Where?'

'Towards the back of the ship.'

A mosaic of sea-containers? He could see those from here. But what else did he have to do with his time other than humour her? Even a half-hour in the stuffy little cabin had done his head in.

'Lead on.'

She led him down the length of the ship and then stopped as she slipped one shoe on from its resting place against a giant blue sea-container. It was only then he realised she'd come to him barefoot. It seemed so comfortable on her he hadn't stopped to think how out of place it was on a working freighter.

'I worried I might not find it again,' she said, her face strangely alight, turning down a gap between the high-rise of stacked containers.

'For someone who takes things so seriously you seem unnaturally delighted by shipping containers.'

She laughed but didn't turn, continuing into the man-made valley. 'Just wait…'

They turned at her next shoe and he began to understand why she'd needed markers. Without the horizon to keep you oriented, this was a maze. She marched onwards then peered to her right—straight into another container from where he stood—

paused and turned back to him, looking for all the world like a delighted child.

Was it a coincidence that he'd only been able to remember her after she'd shed the Shiloh mask?

She grinned at him. 'What's the thing least likely to be around this corner? In the whole world?'

The rapid mental shift that question required took him a moment to adjust. He thought of the craziest and most unlikely thing he could conceive. 'My parents having high tea.'

The delight fell from her face just slightly and her slim fingers rested gently on the edge of the container as she frowned at him. She wouldn't know—about *them*, about why that was such a ludicrous concept, whether they were at sea or not—but she was smart enough to read between the lines.

'I assume it's not that,' he said to cover the silence. To mask his sudden pain.

She straightened and backed up, holding one hand out as though to take his across the emptiness between them, keeping her eyes firmly locked on his. Warm. Beckoning.

A true Siren…

It was only as he stepped towards her that he realised it wasn't a solid wall of sea containers to her left; it was another turn. A turn which opened out to—

'What the—?'

Her face split into a radiant smile and he stumbled to a halt, utterly and genuinely dumbfounded for the first time in his entire life.

A giraffe.

It stood, munching happily on straw and staring at him with a general sort of curiosity as he stood gaping at it. It was housed in the biggest animal crate he'd ever seen, with an opening large enough for it to stretch its long neck and head out of and get a whiff of the sea. A large sort of container clearing had been built around it at the heart of the ship to shelter it from rough weather but give it some sense of air and space.

The strangest sense washed through him—alien and long-forgotten.

Wonder.

Had it really been that long since something had amazed him? Moved him the way those enormous thick-lashed, liquid mercury eyes did. This extraordinary creature standing in this extraordinary place.

Maybe so.

'Back again?' A blonde woman stepped out from behind the crate and murmured quietly to the giraffe before turning her attention to Shirley. She was dressed casually but had the boots and tan of someone who worked outdoors for a living.

'Hayden, this is Caryn,' Shirley said next to him. 'And that—' she nodded at the enormous chomping head fifteen feet above them '—is Twuwu. She's en route to a new home in New Zealand.'

Shirley greeted the woman as he still struggled to find words. En route to a zoo. Of course she was. He'd never had occasion to think about how else you got an animal as big as a giraffe across an ocean.

Shirley went straight into Shiloh mode, asking what were clearly not her first questions of the day, examining the box, leaning back on a tower of containers and just…contemplating. He watched her do her thing but mostly he watched Twuwu. She was so very unconcerned by what was happening around her, content to merely munch on her hay.

'Is she sedated?' he asked.

Caryn turned to him and gave him a winning smile. She was every bit a daughter of nature. Golden-haired, tanned, fit. And interested. Instantly obvious.

'She was lightly sedated for the drive down to the port, and the loading. But she's fully recovered now.'

'She's placid.'

'She's spent a lot of time in that crate preparing for the journey. It's become like her stable.'

He glanced around at the multicoloured wall of containers that surrounded the crate on all sides. 'What would happen if she saw the ocean?'

Again the brilliant smile. Caryn sank on one hip and looked up at him. 'Hopefully we won't find out.'

Shirley rejoined them. 'Will you stay out here for the whole journey?' she asked tightly.

'Most of the day, monitoring her condition, but I'll sleep up in the cabins with everyone else.'

Did she just flick him a glance? Yes, she did.

Well, well...

Shirley continued with her questions and, before long, they knew everything there was to know about international wild-life transactions and the toiletry habits of giraffes. He watched Shirley work—drawing conclusions, filing away every answer for a future story. Eventually all the questions were asked and all the good reasons to be hanging around evaporated.

'You should come back and visit Twuwu during the trip,' Caryn said to Shirley but her eyes flicked to his again. 'She likes company.'

Shirley thanked her and they retraced their steps back through the maze of containers from the heart of the ship to the edge.

'You seem very relaxed.' Just when he thought he liked her best off kilter. Mellow Shirley made him think about long, lazy summer sleep-ins. Naked.

Not appropriate.

'There's something about this ship... Maybe it's the gentle sway... But it chills me out. I find myself relaxing.'

'Maybe it's me?'

Her immediate laugh ricocheted off the containers. 'It's not you.'

Right. Then again, his first instinct on getting her alone in a room with a bed in it had been to paw her. So...

'The giraffe then?' Twuwu had certainly done wonders for his blood pressure.

'Maybe.' They turned out of the massive load of containers at the edge of the ship. 'I'll certainly be visiting again. What an awesome bonus.'

Their next steps passed in silence. Until he couldn't take it any more. 'What do you want to do now?' he blurted.

She turned and blinked at him. 'What do you mean?'

'Us. What will we do now?' And for the next four days.

She laughed and started walking again. 'Don't know about you, but I'm going to start a story for next week.'

He frowned. 'You're working on this trip?'

'Of course. So are you.'

He was supposed to be. But… 'We're in the middle of the ocean. Surely that demands some down time?'

'You've had two years of down time. Are you really so hungry for more?'

No. But he was hungry for something and he couldn't quite put his finger on it. It was an odd kind of…emotional famine. Then it dawned on him.

He wanted company. *Shirley's* company.

'I'm bored. Sea life is interminable.'

She laughed again and jogged ahead of him up the functional steel staircase. He lagged back to appreciate the view. 'We've only been out of the harbour for a couple of hours, Popeye,' she said.

'Entertain me.'

She threw him an arch look back over her shoulder. 'Entertain yourself.'

He thought about Caryn. Then dismissed it. Prodding at Shirley was so much more fun. 'You can write your story when it's dark.'

'I plan to be sleeping when it's dark.'

'Really?' He followed her from the deck into the long corridor that their cabins were in. 'That's a lot of cabin time. What will I do?'

She paused at her door. 'Whatever you want. I have work to do.'

Seriously? She was ditching him? 'Will I see you in the mess room?'

She turned back from unlocking her door. 'Seven p.m. sharp.' She stepped into the room, faced back out at him and leaned on the door. Smiling the way you did to door-to-door salesmen you wanted to get rid of. 'See you then.'

And then she was gone and Hayden stood staring at the flaking paint on the timber, speechless for the second time in a day.

Blonde.

Of course she was. And, in case Hayden hadn't noticed her golden locks, Caryn had tossed them around unmissably. Her skin as tanned as Twuwu's markings and with lashes just as long, too. And all the while *she'd* hovered off to the side, ignored, with her thick hair hauled back in a sea-sensible ponytail and her face virtually make-up-less.

Shirley lay back on one of the two beds in the room and glared at the ceiling. Could it be any more grey or uninspiring?

Could she be any grumpier?

She'd liked Caryn just half an hour earlier. They'd chatted for ages about her work and destination. Then she'd introduced Hayden, picked up on the none too subtle vibe pinging between the two of them and rapidly gone off her.

Not that it was Caryn's fault. She was blonde, gorgeous and willing. Exactly Hayden's type, even if she was wearing steel-capped boots and serviceable shorts and not something slip-thin and expensive. And she herself had been the genius to go and find him and hand him, gift-wrapped, to the only blonde on the freighter. It was entirely self-inflicted.

She sighed.

She'd just... She'd wanted him to have the experience she'd had. The discovery. Coming around that corner and seeing that beautiful animal, so misplaced and unexpected. And she'd enjoyed giving it to him. Everything had gone slow motion just then, as she'd fixed her eyes on his and stepped backward to bring him out into the giraffe's eye line. His face had transformed in that moment, practically glowed, and she had—for precious seconds—a glimpse of the old Hayden. The young man who'd found every aspect of life a revelation. She remembered that face from when she'd hidden under the stairs and watched him through the door crack on Saturdays.

And she'd given him that today.

And then his eyes had refocused on their target—a blonde, the only kind of woman he ever dated—and they'd hardened back into the new Hayden. The Hayden she'd met that very first day at his cottage. The Hayden who was bored with life and out to wring its riches. He hadn't done much else—he hadn't needed to, really, because Caryn seemed happy to carry the burden of the flirting—but her implication was clear.

Come back and visit...

Yay.

She pushed herself onto her side and sat up. Work. She'd said it to get a clean break from Hayden, but suddenly it did seem like a reasonable distraction from her unsanctioned thoughts about *the kiss*. First, unpacking had been a good excuse to stay in here long enough to lose him to his curiosity about how freighters worked. Then roaming the deck and the Lego-stacks of containers.

Now work.

Caryn's chat had triggered a blog idea. About the unseen challenges of international livestock transactions. Zoo animals, racing horses, stud bulls. How many other unique passengers were sitting in crates on ships, planes and trucks around the world right at this moment? It was as unsung as travelling the world on passenger freighters.

She sketched out the preliminary outline of a story and jotted down some research ideas. That neatly took care of...oh... minutes.

'Ugh.' She threw herself backwards and stared again at the offending ceiling. Had they not painted this vessel at all since it was commissioned?

Hayden was responsible for this off-balance mental mess. His incendiary kiss. It had been as unexpected as the giraffe. Though, like the giraffe, once discovered, it was a hard thing to put out of your mind. She'd had to work hard out there on the deck not to keep staring at his mouth. Remembering.

No doubt Caryn the zookeeper would be discovering it very soon.

She'd never met anyone as cynical and miserable as Hayden. That he believed love was a challenge you negotiated rather than something that just struck you... And that he thought it so pathetic that she believed otherwise. That he developed plans for big businesses to better exploit the community.

That was not the boy she'd hidden in the shadows to watch.

The man he'd become might have a full bank account but his moral account was sadly lacking.

Judging him made her feel vaguely better about letting him kiss her.

She forced herself up, back to her laptop, back to the outline of the story she could feel burbling, and verbalised it to tell herself she really meant it.

'Enough.'

A knock at the door ripped her out of the concentrated place where she'd lost time.

'Shirley? It's Hayden.'

Seriously? Could the man not amuse himself for an hour? She had that thought even as her chest tightened around the anticipation. She hit 'save' on her work, stood and yanked the door open. 'Yes?'

He stood there, casually but gorgeously dressed. A clean shirt and well-fitting trousers. Shaved, even. And smelling pretty much like ambrosia.

'Are you coming up for dinner?' he said. 'I thought we were meeting up there?'

She blinked. Half at his appearance and half at what him being showered and shaved meant. 'Now?'

'It's past seven.'

'Right!' How many hours had she lost in her story? That was always a good sign for an engrossing read but not great for saving face in front of Hayden. 'Coming.'

Every instinct called her to put on Shiloh's face—eyes, lips, pallor, carefully chaotic hair—because she'd be meeting strangers, but she remembered her commitment to Hayden and she was determined not to be the one to break faith. On principle. She slipped on her shoes and untwisted the elastic holding her hair back. Sea or not, if tumbling masses were good enough for Caryn…

She raked her fingers through the waves to give it body and then smiled at Hayden. 'Sorry. Let's go.'

Mistake number one.

The wind conditions buried below deck—or even behind a wall of sea containers—and the wind conditions at the top of a freighter were not the same thing. Immediately her hair whipped like silken razors around her face in the gusts, tangling and flying. She wrangled it down as best she could and twisted it in her hold until they reached the outer door of the *Paxos*'s galley. Hayden held the door for her from outside and she stepped through.

Six people turned to look at her—five crew and one zookeeper.

Awesome. Nothing like a subtle entrance.

She blew loose strands from her sea-whipped face and plastered on a smile. 'Sorry I'm late, everyone. I got absorbed in my work.'

She summed up the seating arrangement at a glance. Two empty seats on opposite sides of the table and the one next to Caryn had a half-drunk bottle of Hayden's favourite non-alcoholic beverage in front of it.

Okay…

She moved towards the second vacancy, flanked by the ship's crew.

Introductions were brief, given most of the crew spoke only Greek, but a man she hadn't yet met had good English and proved himself an admirable translator. He was the *Paxos*'s Captain. Just as Greek as the rest of them, just as old and weathered, but somehow more…striking.

Or maybe it was just the uniform.

Hayden sank back into his seat next to Caryn, who immediately drew him back into conversation.

As dinners went, it wasn't the worst she'd had. The food was unexpectedly good and the mood at the table was genial. In fact, the buzz of tension between her and Hayden was the only

thing marring it. He glanced up often, inspired by the boom-
ing laugh of Captain Konstantinos or the smiles of the crew, or
to frown at something one of them said to the other in Greek.
And she did her best to follow along between sips of Australian
wine. Caryn was outstripping her in that regard, putting away
two glasses to her one.

The wine brought immediate colour to Shirley's cheeks in a
Mrs Claus way rather than the appealing slash of colour up the
jaw like it did on the vivacious blonde.

Typical.

Caryn talked and Hayden listened, apparently rapt, and responded on cue. Brief but sufficient. She was certainly doing all
the talking in that little relationship. But then Caryn's conversation was not what he was interested in. Fortunately, it looked
as if she was equally prepared to let body language do the real
talking. She turned three-quarters in to him and leaned forward
to brush or touch him, *a lot*.

Eventually the night and the meal drew to a close and the
crew retired to their bunks or to their shifts. Shirley stood as
the man next to her did and smiled at him. 'Thank you, Captain.
That was lovely.'

He murmured in Greek and then kissed her hand in a sweep-
ing gesture and told her, in English, that the ship's cook had
something suitable for breakfast or lunch at any time they cared
to visit the mess room but that everyone dined together nightly.

'Tomorrow night, then,' she said smiling.

Hayden stood and gave Caryn his arm to help her to her feet.
'Tomorrow night, then,' he echoed brightly.

Maybe if she'd had less wine under her belt Caryn wouldn't
have let the stab of confusion actually show on the outside, but
Shirley saw it as Hayden turned to shake the Captain's hand. She
allowed a momentary pang of sisterhood sympathy; Hayden had
given Caryn his undivided attention for over two hours now suddenly it was 'goodnight'? She shot her a smile she hoped would
be equal parts sympathetic and confederate.

Shirley moved to the door and Hayden crossed to stand behind her, reaching over her shoulder to push it open.

'Batten down the hatches,' he murmured as it gusted open.

The wind had picked up in the time they'd been in the warmth of the Captain's table, so her hair immediately exploded into a tangle around her face. Hayden moved to her other side to help shield her from the worst of it, but all she could do was move as fast as possible back along the deck and down to the floor below where the cabins were, her arms curled around the billowing mess.

She practically fell through the door into the accommodation corridor and he tumbled in behind her. They occupied the few metres to their doors by exclaiming relief at the sudden drop of the elements and then they stood, facing each other, at their respective thresholds.

'I'm coming in,' Hayden announced.

She studied the trace of anger at the corners of his lips. But there was no point fighting it and, truth be told, nine o'clock was rather early to be going to bed, even for her. She opened her door and stood back to give him access and prepared for an onslaught.

'Please, speak to me of something of consequence,' he declared, tumbling like a felled tree onto the second little bed in her room.

The door hung open. It saved her mouth from having to similarly gape. She gently clicked it shut and released the handle. 'You've had nothing but conversation all night.'

'No.' He slid his hands behind his head to replace the pillow she'd stolen to stack on top of her own. 'I've had nothing but yammer all night.'

'She was talking of her home. Her family. Things that were important to her.'

'How could you hear through all the Greek on your side of the table?'

Because she'd been motivated to eavesdrop. And because she'd always been a good lip-reader—a skill she'd perfected under the stairs. 'It was a small table.'

'Longest two hours of my life.'

'That's not fair. If you weren't interested you could have changed the subject.' By the moment, her loyalty was swinging

back Caryn's way. Poor woman. She spent all day in the company of a giraffe and he begrudged her a little verbal offload.
'Or gone wild and contributed to the discussion a little.'

He snorted. 'You think the conversation lacked momentum?
She talked for two hours solid.'

'It wasn't a conversation. She was doing all the work and you
just sat there being enigmatic and mysterious.'

'I wasn't striving for enigma. I was striving for polite.'

Oh, really? 'Was it polite to skip out immediately the food
was taken away?'

'You were about to.'

'I didn't have an offer so clearly on the table.' She balled her
hands at her hips and glared down at him. Suddenly the flirta-
tious Caryn had taken on Everywoman status. And Hayden had
assumed the wrongs of every man who had ever done woman-
kind a bad turn.

He stared at her for heartbeats. She struggled to rein in the
inexplicable heaving of her lungs.

'I wish you could see yourself right now,' he murmured, his
eyes dark and keen.

Her hands immediately went to the disaster that was her hair
and she hated that they'd acted of their own free will. It shouldn't
matter what she looked like. Kiss or no kiss.

'Don't,' he warned. 'You'll ruin it.'

Her fingers paused a breath away from contact, trembled just
slightly. 'Ruin what?'

'All that colour. All that chaos. It's perfect.'

She dropped her hands. 'You think windswept shambles is
the right look for me?'

'I think anything that brings life into your eyes is a good
look. But that one particularly.'

She narrowed her eyes. 'Why?'

He grinned and wriggled in more comfortably. 'If I told you
that, Shirley, you'd throw me out. So how about a new subject?'

A clamp tightened around her organs way down deep inside.
'What if my conversation also fails to meet the rigid standards
of Hayden Tennant?'

'Impossible. You could speak of the weather and I'd find it interesting.'

She stood firm. 'Shall we test that theory?'

The grin graduated into a full smile. 'No. Let's talk about the list. About how we're going to get ourselves up to Queenstown.'

The list. That was safer, yes.

'I don't know.' She shrugged. 'It's an adventure. Let's just see how we go.'

She *should* know. Flying by the seat of her pants was not how Shiloh usually rolled. She really needed to start getting her mind around what would happen beyond the four days with Hayden.

'And so we get there, jump, and then come back to port and these cabins? Seems rather a shame. New Zealand's very beautiful. And romantic.'

'We're not going for the romance. We're going for the adrenalin rush of leaping off a bridge.'

'This doesn't strike me as something Carol would have been into. Needlessly scaring herself witless.'

She sat on her own bed and tucked her legs up next to her. 'I don't think it's about the fear; I think it's about the sensation. The free fall. She might as easily have picked skydiving.'

'I don't see her as a sensation-seeker, either. She was so...'

Shirley lifted a brow. 'Serious?'

He shook his head. 'Cerebral.'

'So bright people trade their right to feel for intelligence? You, of all people, think that?'

He looked up. 'Why "of all people"?'

'Because you're the ultimate sensation-seeker. Or you were.' The photos online showed that.

'Are you saying you think I'm bright?'

She'd thought so once. As brilliant as a polished gem. 'Don't fish for compliments, Hayden. It belittles you.'

'I'd like to know. I know you think I'm disparaging and mean-spirited and idle. It might help balance things out a little if I thought there was any positive in there at all.'

She hadn't called him any of those things out loud so it must have leaked through in her attitude. Natural justice made her confess, 'You were always brilliant, Hayden. And ten years hasn't done anything to diminish that, it seems.'

He considered her. 'For what it's worth, the feeling is mutual.'

She tossed her hair back further from her face. 'It's worth nothing. I don't care what you think of me.'

'Oh, that's clearly not true, or you wouldn't be sitting here twitching to comb your hair.'

Again her fingers betrayed her. She curled them into her fist.

He didn't miss it. His eyes darkened and grew sharp. 'Ask me what I meant when I said this look particularly suits you.'

'No. I don't care what you meant.' And the *thump thump* of her heart was a powerful motivator to silence.

'Yes, you do. You're just too scared to know.'

She glared at him silently.

'I meant that you look like you've just crawled out of a particularly warm and sensual bed.'

Heat instantly returned to her cheeks.

'There it is again. The splash of passion.'

Damn him. She tightened her fists. 'If you'd wanted to play with someone's emotions you should have stayed upstairs.'

'Why can't I just be commenting on fact? You're usually so impeccably presented, so seeing you like this is…stimulating.'

'You should have stayed upstairs for that, too.'

'Are you trying to force me to go knocking on Caryn's door?'

Tension cranked up her spine. 'Actually, no, I don't think she's done anything to deserve the heartbreak you'd inevitably bring.'

One dark blond brow lifted. 'Harsh words, Shirley. You doubt she would understand the concept of a one-night stand?'

'I doubt she'd ever have conceived of what a one-night stand with a man like you might mean.'

The suavadore act dropped. Immediately. The air turned dangerous. 'Meaning?'

Her heart thumped for a different reason then. But she'd started it… 'Meaning it might not be enough for you just to have her and leave. You'd have to break her first.'

He stared. '"Break her"? Is that what you think?'

'It's what you do, Hayden. You take people apart. And you don't always take care to reassemble them again.'

His jaw flexed. 'Have I done that with you?'

He'd done it to year after year of idealistic students on Saturdays. 'I won't give you the chance,' she vowed. 'Ever.'

'Forever's a long time.'

'Fortunately, I have outstanding discipline.'

His smile deepened. 'Oh, yes, you do. But don't you see what that is to a *man like me*?'

She watched him, critically aware that they were alone, in a room full of beds and not much else. And critically aware of what had happened between them the last time they were here. He twisted his body into a seated position, facing her. Closer.

'It's a red rag.'

She lifted her chin. 'I still have free will.'

'I think we've seen how far your free will got you, just this afternoon.'

'I'm not interested in a one-night stand.'

His brow lifted. 'You'd be interested in something longer?'

'No, but that's a moot point. You'd never want something longer.'

'You think not?'

'I know not. If you did you'd have shacked up with any one of those women years ago.'

'What do you have against them? They were all perfectly nice women.'

'Give me one single name.'

He blinked at her.

'Just one, Hayden. If they were so lovely.' She waited. 'I think there's a reason you're so sold on the idea of a love that's intellectual, because it means you can explore the physical with no risk of attachment. Keep the two firmly separate.' She stood. 'But I'm not interested in being your intellectual intimate any more than your physical one.'

Liar!

His face hardened. 'Why not?'

'Because you're too much like hard work. And too risky.'

Blue eyes narrowed. 'What are you risking? Not your heart, which you've firmly stated is inviolate. And not your body, which you protect behind layers of sod-off. So what's left?'

My soul.

'Is this the conversation you were looking for when you came in here tonight?' she gritted.

'No. But maybe it was overdue. I certainly appreciate knowing how you really see me.'

Guilt niggled. 'Hayden, I wouldn't be here with you at all if I thought you were a horrible human being. You're not. But you're not someone that a woman should be backing, emotionally. Not once she gets to know you.'

He reeled back on the bed.

Then he stood. 'Right.'

She stood behind him, stepped towards him. 'Hayden—'

Hayden stopped her with an upheld hand. 'I'll see you in the morning, Shirley.' He got through the door and pulled it shut behind him before breathing again.

Not pity. Not on top of the mouthful of reality she'd already delivered. Just when he thought he didn't have anything soft and squishy left inside, along came Shirley in her metaphorical commando boots and ground what little was left into pulp.

Not once she gets to know you.

Not that he hadn't long suspected it—or could even disagree with it—but something about having it spelled out quite so dispassionately...

By her...

Well, he'd wanted conversation. And one thing he knew about Shirley was that any time spent with her would never go where he thought it would. He'd imagined himself a cosy little scenario that involved the two of them talking long into the night, sharing. Bonding. He'd not let himself imagine anything beyond that, but her wild and dishevelled state over dinner had teased and taunted and distracted him for most of the evening as he'd pretended to listen to Caryn but in fact fantasised about ways of getting Shirley that mussed up himself.

She'd been happily engaged in a long conversation with their trusty Captain about piracy on the high seas—though, given a chance and despite his age, he'd bet his life that the charming Captain Konstantinos would have proven just as untrustworthy with his passenger—and he'd had the double assault of endless monologue on one side and the Shirley Marr show on the other. Complete with seamen who didn't know he understood some Greek discussing with much hilarity the comparative merits of tanned blondes versus sultry brunettes.

The brunettes won.

It wasn't fair to blame Caryn for not being as interesting as the only other woman in the room. The two were completely different people. Night and day. Except he'd spent his entire life indulging in bright, obsequious day when deep down inside he was all about the cool, mysterious night. The cover of night disguised so many more faults.

Shannon. Courtney. Louisa. Dominique.

He had as many names as Shirley could possibly want to hear. It wasn't a struggle with recall that had kept him silent; it was the implication of her words. That he should have started a life with one of them by now. That he was late to some kind of party and that it was his personal failing.

Did she not see the irony?

Shirley had more shields around herself than any man could possibly negotiate. She'd be single and stoic until her last breath, despite her great faith in the random lightning-bolt strike of love.

Who was she to judge his choices?

He reached into his room and grabbed his coat, then headed for the wind storm outside. It was too early to sleep, even if he believed he could. But there was a lot of unexplored ship out there yet.

And a lot of disquiet to burn off.

He wandered the entire circumference of the freighter, staring out through the occasional slot in the bulky siding into the vast nothing of the ocean and up into the vast everything of space. So far from the visual pollution of land, and despite the flood-lights at the front of the ship and the glow of the full moon, the stars seemed to blanket the dark sky. Together they were more than ample to see by.

But one circumference was complete and he wasn't yet ready to return to the solitude of his cabin, which was insane because the past two years had been all about solitude. He turned into the heart of the sea-containers massed in the middle of the vessel.

He heard Twuwu's contented rumination—a kind of chew and snort combo—before he turned the corner into her clearing. A bit of time in the company of a female with no expectations, no opinions and no judgements to cast. That was what he needed.

'Hayden?'

Hell. Awful timing on his part.

'Out for a walk?' Caryn asked. The caution in her voice was immediately obvious and his mind went straight to Shirley's defence of the woman. He sighed.

'Caryn, I think I owe you an apology...'

They talked for quite some time as Caryn finished her checks on Twuwu and settled her for the night. She accepted his fumbled explanation and his assurances of regret for his hasty departure earlier in the evening.

'Is it Shirley?' she asked, wiping her hands on her jeans.

His denial was instant. Too fast. Like his pulse at the mere suggestion of something more going on with him and Shirley. 'It's such a short trip, Caryn...'

She called him on that deflection. 'You don't really strike me as a man who would have a problem with something short-term.'

'I'm not.' At least he wasn't. That thought got him frowning.

'I thought we had a spark.'

And a spark might once have been enough. More than enough. The truth—and the outrage of what it signified— burned. 'It's me.'

She stared at him long and hard. But what could she say, really? Other than the obvious. 'Fair enough. Your loss.'

Maybe so. And given how tightly wound he'd been after storming from Shirley's room, *definitely* so. 'Come on, I'll walk you back.'

'Oh, God, chivalry? You really aren't interested.' She fell in beside him.

It felt good to laugh. And it felt strangely pleasing to have treated this woman with respect. This woman who loved her family and her homeland and was happy to talk to a stranger for hours about them.

'Can I ask you something, Caryn?'

'Shoot.'

'Is your wildlife park anywhere near Queenstown?'

'About four hundred kilometres away.'

Oh. It was worth a shot.

She took pity on him. 'But we go right through Queenstown on the way.'

He lifted his head. 'Will you need any help with Twuwu on the journey?'

She laughed. 'No. There'll be a whole transport team meeting us at Invercargill. Why? You need a lift?'

'It's a long story, but yeah.'

'Let's see what happens. There're always multiple vehicles.'

He held the door of the accommodation deck for her and dropped his voice. 'Thanks. We'll even ride in with Twuwu if we need to.'

'Are you kidding? No one gets to do that.' She stopped a few doors down from Shirley's room. 'This is me.'

He shoved his hands into his pockets, carefully away from her. He wasn't used to negotiating his way *out* of a woman's room. 'I appreciate your understanding, Caryn,' he whispered. 'Considering.'

She laughed in the silence and unlocked her door. 'I think I understand a lot better than you do.'

'See you tomorrow.'

'Yep. Bright and early.' She stepped into her room.

''Night.'

Her door clicked shut. Hayden leaned on the corridor wall and looked diagonally down the hall at Shirley's door. Would she have given him points for that? For extricating himself with care and leaving Caryn's pride intact?

He gave himself a few. And that was rare.

He pushed off the wall and his expensive shoes took him silently down the hall. He opened his door gingerly to avoid waking Shirley. It closed just as quietly.

The entire time he'd paced the ship's deck he'd been working himself up to the decision that he would sleep with Caryn just to show Shirley he didn't care what she thought. To do something with the useless tension resonating through his body and maybe to prove himself as heartless and soulless as she clearly believed. If he was going to burn, it might as well be justified.

Yet here he was, heading to bed solo.

So, all those points he gave himself for treating Caryn with compassion...?

He ripped them off again for being so damn weak.

CHAPTER SEVEN

'So, looks like we're giving you a lift when we head north.' Caryn looked up as Shirley slid into a seat across from her.

'Sorry?'

After a night with no sleep in that tiny dark cabin, she'd been desperate to get out of the confined space that had started to feel like a coffin. Hence her early breakfast. She thought she might have seen some of the crew but she hadn't expected either Caryn or Hayden. Not at this hour. Not after what she'd heard in the hall.

A deep, familiar masculine murmur. A throaty, carefully muted feminine chuckle.

The stone in her stomach settled in further. What had she expected? It wasn't reasonable to tell a man he was worthless and then be shocked when he went out to find someone to prove otherwise.

'When we hit Invercargill,' Caryn clarified. 'Our convoy will go right past Queenstown.'

A ride. She tried to muster up some enthusiasm. 'Oh, great. Thank you.'

'You don't look like backpackers,' she hinted.

So Hayden hadn't told her why they were heading for New Zealand. Shirley didn't know whether to be grateful for his discretion or appalled at his form. He *still* hadn't made actual conversation with her?

What a prince.

A confused jumble of anger and hurt curdled her hastily downed cup of tea. 'We're kind of on a…challenge.'

'You against him?'

Most of the time. 'No. Together.'

'Shame. I could have arranged to leave him behind. We girls have got to stick together.'

Shirley lifted her heavy head. The hint of solidarity confused her. 'He'd only get his wallet out and hire a chopper and be standing there, smug, when we arrived.'

Caryn's eyes grew keen. 'He's loaded then?'

'You could say that.'

She grunted and went back to her eggs. 'Well, that figures.'

'Ladies…'

The man of the moment walked through the door and slid into a seat next to Shirley. Caryn said a cheerful good morning through a mouthful of eggs and Shirley gave a tight smile as the ship's cook came out with two more plates of breakfast and placed them next to each other on her side of the table.

'How did you sleep?' Caryn asked casually.

Shirley reached for the salt and pepper, desperate to be doing something as this conversation happened around her. She concentrated on breathing.

'Actually, like a log,' Hayden said. 'Must be the sea air.'

'Or the late night exercise,' the blonde offered.

Shirley's hand closed hard around the salt shaker. Any harder and it might shatter. 'I'm surprised to see either of you up this early,' she hedged.

'Twuwu has to have checks every four hours overnight,' Caryn said. 'Ten, two and six. So here I am.'

'You went out again after I left you?'

'The line of duty,' Caryn said, wiping her hands and mouth on her napkin. 'I can sleep all I want when I get home.' She stood. 'That said, I'm going to head back down to her now for her six o'clock check. Remember to come on down and say hi. She's bored already.'

'I know the feeling,' Hayden grunted.

Was that why he'd pursued Caryn—*ennui?*

And, ultimately, what did it matter why he'd done it?

You didn't want him, Shirley...

Shirley smiled as Caryn departed, then let it fall from her lips. She focused on pushing her scrambled eggs around the plate.

'You working on a masterpiece, there, Picasso?'

She lifted her eyes to Hayden's. They were lighter, by far, than they had been when she'd last seen him. Maybe his good mood was symptomatic. Unfortunately for him, she'd had no sleep and no...stress relief to enhance her mood. She hit him with full-frontal sarcasm.

'Does arrogance come naturally to you, Hayden, or do you have to work at it?'

His frown doubled. 'Shirley...?'

'Late night exercise. Caryn.'

Duh!

Right at the back of his deep blue eyes a little light bulb illuminated. His answer was measured. 'I walked around the deck and I ran into Caryn on her way back from checking on Twuwu.'

'Unplanned, of course.'

'Yes.'

'Because you know nothing about planning seductions.'

Ha. Hoist with his own petard. And other nautical metaphors.

'There was no seduction.'

'I guess there wouldn't need to be if she was willing enough.'

'There was no sex.'

She pushed her plate away. 'Spare me the details, Hayden. I don't know why I'm so surprised.'

'Given *the kind of man I am*, you mean?'

She rounded on him, guilty heat surging forth. 'Well, was I wrong?'

'Actually, yes, you were. I have nothing to apologise for. And no requirement to, come to think of it. I'm a free agent.'

'So all those murmurings I heard last night were just hallway chit-chat, were they?'

'I have no idea what you heard, but yeah, they would have been.'

A strange kind of earnestness tinged his expression. She frowned. 'You didn't sleep with Caryn?'

'I did not.'

The overhead radio crackled out music but the silence from the kitchen suggested the cook had tiptoed out or was listening in avidly to the raised voices in the mess room. Probably the latter. Maybe he had more English than he let on.

'Right. Okay then.'

Awkward…

His lips twisted but she couldn't honestly call it a smile. 'Apology accepted.' His voice lowered dangerously. 'Now you can tell me something, Shirley… Exactly what business is it of yours what I do? Or with whom?'

She pressed her lips together. 'I… It's not.'

'Insufficient.'

Of course he wasn't going to let her just walk away from having made a colossal ass of herself. He was Hayden. She hissed out a breath. 'You'd just finished telling me how she'd yammered at you all night. So the thought that you'd go straight to her from…' She ran flat out of steam. And courage.

His eyes grew keen. 'Straight to her from you?'

She sat up straighter. 'Straight to her from our argument.'

'No. From you. That's what's bothering you.'

All right, fine. 'You kissed me half to death yesterday and just hours later you were kissing her.'

'Only I wasn't.'

'I didn't know that.' She took a breath. 'It…disappointed me.'

His eyes narrowed. 'I'm sure I disappoint you daily. That's nothing new.'

She didn't answer.

'I have no obligation to you, Shirley. We're friends.' He glanced away. 'If that.'

Ouch. That hurt, unexpectedly. 'We're friends,' she confirmed.

'Then how have I broken faith with you?'

'I just…' What? She had no idea why she had such massive

expectations of him. She sank back in her chair. 'I don't know. I don't know how. I'm sorry.'

The silence in the kitchen slowly returned to the sounds of cooking. Their conversation had apparently become less riveting. Hayden's eyes went from thoughtful to slightly abashed.

'You don't need to beg my forgiveness any more than I need to explain myself to you.'

Friends apologised to friends. Friends explained things to friends.

Not owing him an explanation was a careful way of double reinforcing the fact that they barely even made friend status. As if she'd been clinging to some kind of illusion.

Maybe she had.

Silence resumed.

'How did you go for Internet signal yesterday?' he asked, finally breaking it.

'Good. The ship has a router on the accommodation deck. The Wi-Fi is good.'

'Great.'

Awesome. Talking about Internet signal strength. Only marginally less pathetic than talking about the weather.

'Does that mean you're going to be working today?' she checked.

'I think I might. Up here in the recreation area. See what I can get done.'

Was she surprised he was in no hurry to hang out with her? Or even near her. 'Okay. Good luck with that.' She stood. 'I'm going to head off for a shower.'

'Catch you later, then.'

And less enthusiastic words had never been spoken. She noticed the careful way he studied the watery horizon.

Lord.

It was going to be a long four days.

CHAPTER EIGHT

THE CONVOY pulled away and rumbled off into the distance, leaving Hayden and Shirley standing on the edge of the Gibbston Highway, daypacks in their hands. Twuwu's massive head poking out the back of the trailer grew smaller and smaller in the distance until she pulled it back inside her crate.

Shirley did a slow three-sixty, taking in the dramatic view around them. This part of New Zealand's South Island was a topographer's delight, all ancient ranges and green river valleys with turquoise water lying far below. On the horizon, snow-capped mountain peaks were protected by a layer of white cloud.

'So, here we are,' she breathed.

'They're expecting us?'

'They know we're coming today, just not when.'

And thanks to Caryn and Twuwu being the first piece of freight off the *Paxos*, they were hours ahead of what she'd forecast.

They started walking towards a distant car park to check in. Beyond that was an old steel and stone suspension bridge that forded the river rushing by fifty metres below. And dotted all over that were people. Everywhere. Even though it wasn't yet mid-morning.

A long scream punctuated the serenity like the cry of an eagle soaring overhead, chased, moments later, by cheers and whistles.

She sucked in a breath.

Hayden glanced at her. 'Nervous?'

Until that moment, she hadn't been. She'd been way too busy

being distracted by Hayden's emotional withdrawal. But given how her body reacted to simply walking up the *Paxos*'s gang-plank, she suddenly doubted whether she'd be able to step out into the nothingness of open space at all.

Cord or no cord.

Fear was not a good way to get something like a bucket list achieved. She blew the breath out carefully. 'I guess we'll find out.'

The organisers slotted them in after the present batch of jumpers had gone through. They waited for the first hour on the observation deck, which hung out high above the gorge, amongst the friends and families of those taking the leap. As the morning wore on, the deck got more and more slippery as those taking the plunge climbed back up the side of the valley, wet, and then joined the spectators to vicariously relive their experience.

'That's a good sign,' Hayden murmured close to her ear. 'If it was traumatic I doubt people would stick around to watch others going through it.'

Trauma. Something else she hadn't thought about. She'd been so focused on how she was going to get out there at all she hadn't really thought about whether or not she'd ever recover from it.

The growing spectator crowd pressed them closer together and Hayden slid an arm around behind her to keep the soggiest of them back. Soon enough they were funnelled out of the crowded area to the two ornate stone towers that anchored the bridge to the land at both ends. A production line of safety instructions and advices began there and Shirley busied herself with taking them very seriously and making an endless stream of decisions.

'Single or tandem?' the young man in the bright T-shirt asked.

'Single,' she said. Just as Hayden said, 'Tandem.'

She looked at him. He lifted an eyebrow. 'Do you seriously think you're going to be able to do this alone?'

She glanced over the edge of the bridge at the sparkle of blue water so very far below. Not as far as in the movies, but far enough to kill you if you got it wrong. There was a couple jumping together as she watched and it wasn't…intimate…in the way tandem skydives were. They just stood next to each other.

Until they plunged, of course.

She dragged her eyes back to the young man. 'Tandem. Thank you.'

'Bob, touch or full immersion?'

'Uh...' It was like ordering a pizza. Mozzarella or feta? She glanced at Hayden, lost.

'You want to get wet?' he translated.

No. She didn't want to do this at all, as it turned out. But her mum would have wanted the full splash-down experience. 'Full immersion?'

Hayden smiled at her uncertainty and murmured, 'That's my girl.'

They shuffled forward. Only one station from the one with rubber ropes involved. Oh Lord...

A girl met them this time, even younger than the first and with a heavy Welsh accent. She took them through the safety talk again and outlined the procedure for getting out of the water at the bottom.

'Relax,' Hayden murmured in her ear.

Her tight throat translated into a squeaky voice. 'This place is run by child backpackers...'

He laughed and shuffled her forward, right to the opening on the side of the red iron bridge. It wasn't glamorous—far from it—but the men doing the tying on at least did look as if they'd been shaving for longer than a year.

Ahead of them a young woman jumped, and then a fifty-something man.

Surely if someone with silver hair could do it then she could do it?

A heavily tattooed arm waved them forward.

Her feet locked to the bridge as surely as if they had been bolted there. 'I can't do it.'

Hayden looked back. 'Yeah, you can. Look how much trouble you've gone to getting here.'

She pressed back against the side of the suspension bridge. 'It doesn't matter. I can't do this.'

Behind Hayden, the man lowered his arm and started to-wards them. She instinctively curled her fingers into Hayden's shirt in case the big guy just picked her up and threw her over. His arms immediately curled around her. 'What about you just step out there with me. Take a look?'

She'd been looking all this time—what was going to change about it out there? She shook her head.

'Come on, gorgeous.' The operator smiled, reaching them. 'It's not as bad as it looks. You've got a fourteen-year-old behind you.'

She turned to check on the veracity of that. Sure enough, a toothy kid smiled back at her.

'Is this your first time?' she asked.

He shook his ginger hair. 'Fourth. It's cool.'

She looked back to Hayden. 'There you go,' he said. 'It's cool.'

She didn't want to be cool; she wanted to be alive. Then, right hard on the heels of that thought, came another one—they were doing this in the first place to *feel* alive. To experience life in all its forms.

Including its terrifying ones.

Her foot peeled off the deck.

'That's the way,' the operator said and whistled for his compatriot, who hung two large white lengths of rubber rope on their bollards.

Hayden curled his fingers through hers and led her forward.

'Aren't you scared?' she whispered up at him.

'Yep. But I'm not about to let you see that. On principle.' He winked at her. 'Anything Shiloh can do, I can do.'

Shiloh. She could do it.

She let herself be shuffled out onto a platform fixed to the side of the bridge and she let the safety lesson wash over her. Something about the little yellow boat that would come for them when they were done and about keeping your feet together.

As she heard the words, someone snapped two thick blue straps around her ankles like fabric handcuffs, forcing them together. Then they did Hayden's. It meant they could shuffle but not walk out onto the timber dive-boards that got them clear of the bridge. One was skinny, the other wider. For two.

Hands guided her out onto the wide one and Hayden shuffled up next to her.

'Okay?' His glance held genuine concern. 'Ready?'

Her chest tightened so hard she could barely get a word out.
'No.'

'To which?'

'To both.' The blood rushed past her ears the way the river
below them roared down the gorge.

'Take a second, Shirley,' he whispered close to her ear.
'Appreciate where we are.'

She forced her head up, away from the milky-blue water deep
below, forced herself to think about where they were and what
they were doing. How extraordinary it was. How stunning the
landscape was.

'Look at me...'

She brought her eyes back to his. They were the same blue
as the tumbling water below. For one fanciful moment that actually made all this better because falling from a great height
into Hayden's eyes was something she could easily imagine.
And not imagine hating.

Her pulse settled just a fraction.

'This is for your mum,' he said. He lifted the hand that she
hadn't realised he still had clasped in his. 'We're doing this because she couldn't. And I really can't imagine a time or a place
that we could possibly be closer to her than here, doing this
crazy wrong thing. Look around and tell me that gods didn't carve
these mountains, that angels don't roost amongst those trees.'

She did, and she couldn't.

'We're going to step out together, Shirley, into this magical,
mysterious air. And it's going to glide us down safely to the boat
below like God's breath.'

She stared up at him, her icy fingers clenched tightly in his,
breathing as fast and shallow as she had after their kiss. Every
single thing she knew about him and his past evaporated in that
moment and he was just a man she trusted, a man she admired.
A man heavy with flaws but so very heavy with brilliance, too.

A man who could get her through this and any other challenge she ever had in life.

She smiled, even if it did wobble. 'You're so full of it, Tennant.'

His head dropped and his smile broke sunlight across the whole valley. 'But did it work?'

She looked inward. Her pulse had leveled out, her breathing had eased and even the distance below them seemed to compress into something survivable. This was just like jumping off the high board back in school.

A really, really high board.

She turned and faced outwards, keeping her hand curled in his. 'It worked.'

Behind them the tattoo guy counted down.

Five...four...

When he got to three, Hayden turned suddenly, bent and pressed his mouth to hers, hot and hard.

One.

Gravity tore their lips apart as they fell forward, free and fast, and her stomach heaved. The sound coming out of each of them was much the same, just harmonised. Then the straps around her ankles tightened into a fabric vice and her free fall arrested and she was dunked bodily into the Kawarau River before being yanked out again and hurled back into the air like a rag doll.

Her smaller size meant she bounced in opposition to Hayden, laughing and sobbing and crying out to the gods that she'd just defied by surviving such a fall. Life coursed through her veins like the drug it was, and she simultaneously felt the exact position of every cell in her body. Every decision in her life suddenly grew acutely clear—the wrong turns and the right. Above her dangling self she saw the yellow pickup boat moving into position and the pressure of her full weight on her ankles started to bite. Her hair pointed in long, straight, drenched shards to the earth.

'Oh, my God!'

She turned to face Hayden, hanging upside down like Spiderman next to her. He reached out a hand, stretched out a finger and snagged one of hers, pulling her close as the pickup guys hooked her bungee with a boat hook. It took only a minute to pull them down into the boat and release the ankle boots. She fell, as heavy and inelegant as a load of fish from a dragnet, into the base of the boat. Hayden sprawled in next to her. Their cords vanished back up into the sky.

There were no words.

There was no past and no future.

There was no one in the world but them.

She twisted in the puddle on the floor of the boat and threw her arms around Hayden, overcome. Their wet, heated bodies fused together along with their lips. His hands bunched in her wet hair and pulled it out of the way so that his mouth could raze her own. She sucked in his air and his smell and the very flavour of him and pressed herself more fully against him, desperate for more. Wondering how she'd survived this long without ever feeling this.

Her head spun more now than during her free fall.

He twisted her into him and dragged her across his lap as the little boat began to move to the edge of the gorge. She fed off his heat and gasped at the furnace of his touch.

It was the gasp—or maybe the touch—that drew a tactful throat-clear from one of the two men running the boat. 'Adrenalin,' he volunteered. 'We get this a lot.'

She immediately stiffened and went to pull away but Hayden simply lifted his lips and pulled her back to lie in the soggy bottom of the dinghy, staring at the sky. Together. His heart hammered right below her ear where she rested on his chest. Hers matched it. It hadn't stopped pounding since she'd first stepped onto the bridge all the way up there, and it was still repeating as hard as their outboard motor now.

As she lay there using Hayden as a pillow, the cadence of the thumps and the punctuation of his breaths formed a hypnotic blanket. Slowly...so slowly...her pulse eased, her breath returned and her mind was quiet.

'Land ho,' one of the two men said as the dinghy bumped against the edge of the gorge. She would have scrambled out anyway but it was doubly tough in saturated clothes that clung and inhibited her progress.

What was it with her and Hayden? She seemed to be forever plucking sodden garments from her body when he was around. This time she didn't bother. If he wanted to stare at her wet butt as he followed her up the long, steep trail back to the top of the gorge he could knock himself out.

It wasn't as if they were strangers any more. Not after that kiss. Or the one before it.

'Retinas intact?' she asked, back over her shoulder, when she should have been apologising for launching herself on him.

He laughed through the puff of scaling the gorge wall. 'So far so good.'

The climb became torture, so close behind the chemical rush of the jump and the muscle collapse of recovery, and took all her strength and air. Conveniently, it also excused her lapse into silence.

She used the time to think.

What had just happened?

He might have kissed her briefly at the top of the jump but it had been more of a solidarity kiss, a kiss for courage. What they had just shared splayed out in the bottom of the boat, despite the audience, was something else altogether. Something far more dangerous.

And she'd started it.

The adrenalin, of course. The skipper of the pickup boat had excused it as much. In that moment she'd needed nothing more in the entire world than someone to connect with. But would she have done that with some stranger that she'd just met?

No.

This was about Hayden.

She'd felt it when she'd first walked up to him at his cottage and he'd looked at her with such sultry interest. She'd felt it surrounded by children, crouched across a suburban battlefield from Leonidas, and doubly so when they'd lain in the sun drying. She'd definitely felt it when he'd kissed her half to death to make his point just a few nights ago.

All of those moments were just leading to the one they'd just shared in the boat.

And he knew it.

You started to buy in to me touching you months ago…

He'd warned her. He'd told her how his vision of strategic seduction worked. Why should she be surprised, now, to discover his manipulations were working?

Except…was it manipulation if you really wanted it?

If you started it?

Then again, wasn't that one of the key principles of his theory? Convincing her it was her idea all along.

She emerged at the top of the gorge slightly ahead of him and didn't wait. She struck out across the car park, shaking her head briefly at the staff member waiting at the top to upsell a second jump.

Seriously? People could do it again after just a short break?

'Shirley…'

She kept moving.

'Are we jogging back to the ship?'

That slowed her. Where exactly did she think she was going? She had to face him sometime.

'Stop.' A strong hand curled around her upper arm and drew her to a halt.

She let him pull her into a standstill, smack bang in the middle of the car park out here in the middle of nowhere. Halfway back to the locker that held their daypacks.

She spun on him. 'What?'

'We kissed. It's not the end of life as we know it.'

Not for him, maybe. The chances of her ever forgetting how she'd felt with her skin merging with his? Not high. 'It wasn't what I wanted.'

'You kissed me.'

'I know!' That was what was so infuriating. And confusing. 'It doesn't mean anything.'

Again, not for him, maybe. She lifted her eyes. 'It means your stupid games worked.'

He wasn't about to pretend he didn't understand. A tiny part of her acknowledged the respect that hinted at. 'I thought it was a pretty good way to cap off an amazing experience.'

'That's because it wasn't your mother we were doing this for.'

She frowned. How had her mother come into this all of a sudden?

'No. We're a decade too late for my mother. And she never had a bucket list. She was too busy surviving.'

A car tooted politely behind them and Shirley realised they were standing in the middle of the vehicular thoroughfare. She stepped back, away from Hayden, and he did the same. The car progressed through.

'What do you mean?' she asked when he stepped back up next to her.

His eyes stayed fixed on the building their lockers were in. But he avoided her question. 'You can't use your mother as a shield every time we start getting close.'

She stiffened. 'I don't.'

'Yeah, Shirley. You do.'

'Then we see it differently.'

He hissed his frustration and she turned and kept walking. 'I'll tell you how I see it,' he said, catching up with her. 'We have massive chemistry but, instead of indulging it and working it out of our systems, we go head to head constantly and leak it out that way.'

'Speak for yourself,' she muttered.

'I am speaking for myself. I just stand near you, Shirley Marr, and my cells start twitching. If that little boat had been slower and emptier and if what I wanted was the only thing that mattered, then you and I would be having sex right now instead of standing up here getting our kicks verbally.'

'You make a lot of assumptions, Tennant.'

'You're lying if you say you don't feel it.'

She spun again. 'I don't *want* to feel it.'

He snorted. 'I get that, loud and clear. It must infuriate you to find yourself attracted to *a man like me.*'

'Oh, will you let that go? I was angry.'

'You're always angry, Shirley. And it's getting pretty old.'

She stared at him, shuffling through all the words available to her and none of them seemed adequate. Except maybe the truth.

'You're not safe, Hayden,' she whispered, pressing her fingers to her left breast. 'For me.'

The rapid change of direction had him shaking his head. He took a moment to choose his words. 'Life isn't safe, Shirley. But you have to live it or you might as well not bother.'

'Like you haven't been for the past few years?'

His eyes didn't waver. 'Yeah. Exactly like that. I was just taking up air.'

Her lips pressed together. But on some level she recognised his use of the past tense. 'Why?'

'No.' He shook his head. 'You don't get to have it both ways, Shirley. You can't keep me locked at arm's length but then expect me to share myself with you.'

'Is that why you never have close relationships? So you don't have to share yourself?'

His jaw tightened and his skin seemed to drop colour. 'The bus is coming.'

She followed his eyes and, sure enough, the hourly shuttle bus back to Queenstown was trundling over the traffic bridge that spanned the Kawarau River.

They turned for the locker area and retrieved their property. Shirley checked in briefly with the owner and got a contact for a later interview on the history of this insane sport, then jogged across the asphalt and climbed onto the waiting bus.

Hayden sat three-quarters of the way back, staring out of the window. Expression closed. As she approached, she saw that his bag occupied the empty seat next to him.

Right.

She pivoted on her feet and returned to a seat immediately behind the driver and promptly engaged him in a conversation long enough to pass the entire trip back to Queenstown.

The driver radioed ahead and arranged with the departed Invercargill bus to slow its progress long enough for them to intercept it on the highway. They did a quick roadside bus-swap and found themselves heading south. This time Hayden left the seat next to his open and she sank into it wordlessly. She pulled out her notepad and made some fast notes from her discussion with the driver and then busied herself admiring the stunning scenery as they travelled south to the coast. Out of the window, away from Hayden. But the whole time he dominated her thoughts. Him and the heated moments in the boat.

They cleared port immigration and headed for the waiting *Paxos*.

'Welcome back,' the crewman they'd first met said as she hurried up the gangway. Not because the ship was waiting to leave but because she couldn't wait a moment longer to get a nice solid door between herself and Hayden.

So much hung, unsaid. Yet they'd also said too much. How could both be true?

He led them back up to the accommodation corridor and turned to them with a flourish.

'Two rooms,' he announced in passable English, clearly pleased with himself.

They'd had to surrender their rooms on arrival for immigration reasons but their bags sat waiting neatly in the hallway outside their previous accommodation. Shirley stared at her bag as though she were seeing it for the very first time.

Hayden's words back up at the gorge whooshed through her head.

Life isn't safe.

She could spend the next few months running from the feelings that were growing more confusing and more intense by the day, or she could turn and face them. On her own terms. Maybe she could control it if she was driving it.

Or die trying.

'One room,' she heard herself saying past a dry mouth.

The crewman's lined face wrinkled further. Hayden's eyes swung her way.

'One room?' the two men said together.

She locked eyes with Hayden. Shock filled them. And that was pretty rare in the Master of the Impassive. She lifted a brow. Took a breath. 'Any objections?'

Five little syllables that changed so very much.

He stared at her, a question live in his blue eyes. The crewman glanced between them, still uncertain.

'One room.' Hayden nodded.

In a flourish of reproachful Greek, the crewman collected her bag and Hayden's and swung the door to his old room open and placed the suitcases inside. Then he turned and stomped off. Shirley followed Hayden in, her heart wringing every single drop of blood out of its tight chambers. He spun around to face her as soon as she clicked the door shut behind them. And locked it.

'You have to live life or you might as well not bother,' she quoted, bolder than she felt.

Suspicion lined his handsome face. 'You didn't want this.'

'I still don't.' He frowned. She swallowed slowly, dampened her lips. 'So why do I? So very badly?'

Then she was moving. And so was he. They came together in the middle of the tiny room, all hands and lips and tongues and clumsy haste. Hayden pressed her up against the locked door and plundered with his tongue, forking his fingers into her hair and yanking it roughly out of its elastic band. She did the same with his T-shirt from the band of his shorts. It was still damp from their river dunking and bus travel. But freeing it meant she could slide her hands around his searing flesh and mould the refined, lean contours of the back she'd glimpsed when he was Leonidas as he pressed into her hard from the front.

'It's like the surf at night,' he murmured, nuzzling his face into the dark waves of her hair and breathing fire into her ear. She smiled at the poet still in him, knowing well what it must really look like after their adventures today, and tipped her head back as far as the door behind her would allow so that he could suck and bite his way across her throat.

Then he returned to her mouth, pressing short and long kisses into her receptive flesh as he ground his hips into hers. 'I've wanted to do this since you first sat in my living room all prim and proper and with boots fastened up to your knees.' His hands left her hair and traced a path down to her waist. 'I wanted, then, to unlace you one eyelet at a time. This will have to do.'

Her dark maroon shorts were a surf brand, tied at the top for effect. He impatiently yanked each lace free of its eyelet and then pulled her backwards towards the two tiny beds. He released her only long enough to get behind one while she got behind the other and they pushed them together, the momentum flinging them back into each other's arms as they met in the middle.

She kneeled on her side of the bed, stretching up to find his mouth again, breathing heavily. Gasping as she had in the boat. Overwhelmed by her own audacity. And need.

He fisted his fingers in her hair and tipped her head back, away from his lips, until her heavy glance lifted and focused on his.

'Are you sure, Shirley?'

She was sure that she'd never felt this swirling, uncontrollable need in her life. She was sure this moment would never come again if she stopped it now. She was sure that people had survived entire lifetimes on a single glance, a touch, and that just wasn't going to be enough for her.

Was she sure…?

'No,' she breathed. 'But I'm doing it anyway.'

He circled her with his arms and twisted her below him, lying at right angles across the rift between the twin beds, pressing down hard and hot on top of her and gently finding her lips with his. If he'd come on heavy just then—seducer Hayden—she might have baulked, the intensity of feeling soft mattress below her and solid man above just a little bit too real. But he didn't; he timed his switch to explorer Hayden just perfectly—long, leisurely, lazy—and it sucked her into a place where the room spun gently and her breath shallowed out, and the only thing that wasn't spinning or stealing oxygen was right in front of her.

Hayden.

Heavy and protective lying across her. Stroking her hair back from her damp face, taking his time, getting to know her, his blue eyes creating an anchor for her out-of-control emotions. He levered himself up onto one hand and stripped his shirt off with the other, watching her closely the whole time. Waiting for her to freak out and change her mind. Waiting for her to follow suit.

She lay there, breathing heavily as his eyes raked her body. Flat out refusing to back out now. Just when she was getting everything she didn't know she wanted.

'You want some help getting those off?' he whispered, his eyes darkening dangerously and his fingers tracing down her shirt to her unlaced shorts.

'What?' She gasped at his fingers low against her belly and forced herself to focus.

'Your shorts. Your shirt.'

She sucked her lip between her teeth and breathed, 'You want them...?'

His body answered for him. His eyes darkened. 'I want what's inside them.'

She locked eyes on his and smiled—determined, desire-heavy, defiant—and then purred two magical words into the air between them.

'*Molon labe.*'

CHAPTER NINE

COME and take them.

Boy, had he. He'd practically torn them in his haste to get them off her, to strip off all the final trappings of Shiloh and get back to the raw essence of Shirley.

Raw.

The right word. That was how they'd been long into the evening. They'd missed the captain's supper—*bad passengers*—and he'd had to sneak up to the galley late that night to guilt the cook into bundling together a few things for them to eat. To refuel.

A few hours later they'd fallen asleep, slick and spent and wrapped in each other's scent in the pushed-together bed.

And now it was morning. And Shirley was stirring.

Hayden used the last precious moments of her oblivion to scan her face once more. Free of make-up, free of stress, free of any kind of judgement. Greedy, guilty, stolen moments. He lifted a single lock of dark hair from her face with his little finger.

Her eyes fluttered open, confused. But they cleared again a heartbeat later as she remembered what they'd shared the night before.

He put on his game face. 'Good morning.'

She stretched like a cat under the sheets. Winced. Then blushed at the reason for the wince. Then smiled.

A smile. *Could've been worse.*

'Morning,' she murmured.

'Hungry?'

'Ravenous.'

'Want to head up to breakfast?'

'In a bit.'

He nodded. 'Want first run at the bathroom?'

She shook her head. 'Let me wake up first.'

'Want to talk about what changed between Queenstown and the docks?'

He didn't mean to say it, didn't even know he wanted to ask it until the words tumbled off his lips. He wasn't in the habit of questioning—or pushing—his luck.

She watched him steadily. 'Other than the scenery?'

'Ha ha.'

She sat up and kept the sheet tucked carefully under her arms. That seemed a crime now that he knew from first-hand experience what was under there. The memory of her skin sliding against his was still so fresh.

She shrugged. Slowly. 'I just decided that casual sex shouldn't be merely a male prerogative.'

His gut tightened. 'Casual as in one-off?' It hadn't felt very casual as she'd writhed under him and clenched her long fingers into his flesh.

She arched a brow. 'I think we're already over our quota for that, don't you?'

Point.

'Casual as in...casual,' she went on. 'Not a big deal. Something nice to do when we see each other.'

Nice. He stared at her, not letting the twist in his belly grow into anything harder. 'Those might just be the last words on the planet I ever expected to come out of your mouth.'

She leaned back against the wall and kept her eyes guarded. 'Maybe I've found myself at sea.'

Or lost yourself. And he had a nasty feeling he might have been responsible for that.

Shouldn't he be celebrating now? He'd got to have sex with Shirley. Shirley-the-untouchable. She'd let him touch her wherever he wanted last night. Repeatedly.

A man like you...

Had he dragged her down to his level?

Her scowl returned and that, too, was a crime after the ec-stasy that he had seen stamped on her features last night. 'Relax, Hayden. You haven't corrupted me. I'm here because I wanted to be.'

Had she meant to use the past tense?

And…by the way…could he *be* more of a teenage girl about this?

He gave himself a mental punch. *Come on.* This was what he did. He had sex with beautiful women, enjoyed them in the moment, kissed them goodbye and moved on. Occasionally he came back for round two but never round three. On principle.

Moments like this were not new to him. But this…disquiet certainly was.

This felt all kinds of wrong.

He glanced at naked, make-up-less, alabaster-skinned Shirley. Carol-Anne's little girl. But he would totally have hit on her way back when she'd sat in his living room like a gift from the gods of sensuality if he'd thought he had a chance, and he'd known *then* who she was. So it couldn't just be about her genes.

This was about her.

He was uncomfortable because it was *her*.

Shirley. The person. The woman. The soul.

He pushed to his feet. 'I might just grab a shower.' It was down the hall. A decent physical separation so that he could think.

Khaki eyes tracked him silently as he pulled on jeans and a T-shirt over his nothingness and bundled up some clean under-wear and a towel. That beautiful mind turning slowly over. It made him nervous. But he made himself turn back and smile. Just because he was wigging out didn't mean he had to show it.

'Back in a tick.'

She nodded and he was gone. The one bathroom on the floor was small but serviceable and, given how few of them there were on this skeleton-crew voyage, it was in reasonable condi-tion. He stripped off again and stepped under the spray before it was fully warm.

Shirley hadn't responded to him as if she was caving under

pressure. On the contrary, she'd taken the lead. She'd been more than decisive at his door yesterday afternoon. Far more than he'd managed. All he'd done this trip was moon around feeling misunderstood. Last night Shirley had been a wake-up call. A healthy reminder that short, passionate affairs were his past and his future. And roughly what he had a right to expect, given the kind of man he was. If she'd gone on being enigmatic and chaste and so bloody *uninterested* he might have started getting unhealthily obsessed. Clouded and off-track. Started doubting the lessons of his life.

He was a man who did best with his emotions firmly holstered.

She was a woman who had impeccable timing and a sense of the dramatic. Just because she played him better than most didn't mean it wasn't still a play. Hell, he admired her all the more for it. That kind of sense for people would do very well at his firm. Below the intrigue and the professional disguise, Shirley was a woman just like any other—infinitely less inhibited as the night wore on and she let herself open to him—and hard to walk down the hall away from. But basically made of the same cloth.

And, frankly, he was relieved.

If she'd been cut from any other fabric he might have had a much harder time walking away from her. Not just down the hall to the shower but *away*.

He built himself a decent soap lather and then slopped it everywhere that mattered. Rather more roughly than was warranted.

Again—why wasn't he celebrating? He had a gorgeous, flammable woman in his bed offering him a no-strings out, and the significant pleasure that he gleaned from being right. Last night had been in their future from the first time she had let him touch her.

So why would he really rather be wrong?

Shirley let her breath out slowly and evenly as Hayden's footsteps diminished with distance. She sagged back against the wall.

What was she doing?

Had she truly gone all *friends-with-benefits* on him? Hayden? The man who'd made an art form of the one-night stand? As if there was any other way of doing things in his head. She might just as likely wander up to the bridge of the *Paxos* and tell Captain Konstantinos the difference between port and starboard.

Part of what she'd said was true—she was here because she wanted to be. But he'd looked so earnest when he'd asked her what had changed after Queenstown, and then so *sick* when she had assured him how much she wanted to be here.

Way to play all your cards at once, Shirley.

But done was done. And there were worse outcomes, for her, than having him believe none of this was a big deal. Though it was. A very big deal. She might have made her decision suddenly but she hadn't done it lightly. She knew exactly what she'd be sacrificing by being with him. But she hoped her dignity would be partially salvaged by making it clear that them being together was not because of any *influence* he'd applied, but because it was her choice. What she wanted.

And was it ever.

She'd stood there in the corridor and tried to imagine them going to their separate rooms and maintaining a careful distance all the way back to Australia, the way they had on the way out. And she couldn't do it. Too much had passed between them.

She'd hung, upside-down, from that old bridge and curled her fingers around his as he pulled her into his strong orbit and she'd known there and then that they would be together one way or another.

Her subconscious just hadn't updated the rest of her until the last moment.

And maybe it had been wise not to if it had had a clue of the ferocious charge that would surge between them once she opened the proverbial floodgates. The moment her decision had been made and his lips had touched hers…she'd been lost.

Lost enough to still feel it now.

Lost enough to want more the moment he got back.

But sane enough not to let it show.

Ever.

Four days back seemed to take half the time of the journey east. Maybe it had something to do with the ocean currents or trade winds, or the way time altered when she was with Hayden. And how it lagged when they were apart. Which wasn't often. They slept together, they ate together, they walked together, they worked together.

A whole lot of together considering they were two very un-together type people. But having no right to claim on someone was strangely liberating. Either of them could walk out of the door at any moment and the other would have no fair cause for complaint.

But something kept them tethered to each other like they had been up at Kawarau gorge.

Maybe it was knowing that as soon as the boat docked in Sydney—this moment, now—their relationship would be over. Their *thing*. No legitimate reason to be with each other any longer. Until next time. A few more precious, extraordinary days.

Shirley turned and peered up the vast hull of the docked *Paxos*. She waved back at Captain Konstantinos on the bridge. Funny how rapidly friendships formed when you took meals together.

Going back to eating alone was going to be tough.

She turned back to Hayden, standing on the dock. Funny how rapidly friendships formed when you took pleasure together, too. The past four days had been the shortest and longest of her life. He'd liberated parts of her she'd never met before and let her get closer than she could ever have imagined getting to him. Not all the way in, but part way.

For him, she sensed, that was a lot.

'So…' He swung around to face her once they were clear of the busy port activity.

She smiled up at him brightly, determined not to let anything show. 'So…'

'I guess that's it then?'

Did he have to sound so relieved? 'Guess so.'

'Until next time?'

Right. The list wasn't done yet. That meant neither were they. 'The next one's yours,' she breathed. And that meant the ball was in his court. If he didn't want to see her again then he only had to drag out organising the next list item.

She wasn't going to beg.

He looked away, watched a dispute between forklifts nearby. Then he brought his eyes back to her. 'I really enjoyed New Zealand. The journey. Our time together.'

Lord... Were all casual things this awkward to walk away from? 'Yeah, it was fun.'

And intense and challenging and scary and deeply moving all at the same time. But 'fun' just seemed safer to go with under the circumstances.

'Thank you,' he finally said. The first honest thing to come from his mouth.

'What for?' Throwing herself at him or not making a scene about their parting?

'For letting me come on this journey with you.'

'I know you probably would have been more comfortable on one of those.' She nodded at yet another cruise liner berthed across the harbour. And suddenly she was imagining being with him in an opulent suite with a spa bath and a king-sized bed and a really plush, really comfortable carpet.

'Maybe, but it wouldn't have been nearly as memorable. Actually, I was thanking you for letting me in on this whole journey to fulfil the list. It's been—' he struggled for the right word '—good for me. To have direction. Purpose.'

That was such a profound thing to say twenty seconds before they parted ways.

Unless...

It wasn't too profound for a goodbye statement. It would be just like Hayden to seek closure with some grand gesture. Maybe he wouldn't follow up with the next list item after all.

She stretched up and kissed him on the cheek. Ridiculously chaste. Determined to save him the trouble of ending things.

'Goodbye, Hayden. I'll see you—' *Soon? Later? In my dreams?* She didn't have control over any of them, so she just settled for, 'I'll see you.'

'I'll be in touch.'

Which was just one step removed from *'I'll call you.'*

She had no experience with the whole friends-with-benefits thing. What was the protocol here? Cool, aloof and *take it as it comes?* Or warm, open and *on like Donkey Kong the next time I see you?* She was almost certain it wasn't *throw your arms around him and beg him to stay.*

That burning urge couldn't be good for anyone. And, as she'd once bragged, her strongest trait was supposed to be her self-discipline.

She turned for the long-stay parking and reached for her bag. He bent for it at the same time and their fingers tangled on the handle. He straightened, his eyes locked on hers. He relinquished the bag.

'I'll be in touch,' he repeated. Somehow his intense eye contact was like an elaborate signature at the bottom of a legal document. So she knew he meant it.

She smiled. Turned. Left.

Walking away was even harder than stepping off the platform up in the gorge. At least then she'd had the press of his hot, urgent lips to distract her.

Now she had nothing.

CHAPTER TEN

'I AM almost certain this is not what my mother had in mind.'

Six weeks. Six weeks after the *Paxos* had berthed in Sydney and swapped her half-empty cargo for a full complement and left two passengers standing on the dock.

Six long weeks without seeing Hayden.

But she wasn't about to betray her excitement.

The two of them wobbled horribly in a dug-out canoe ten feet from the jetty sticking out from the immaculately crafted but soulless canal suburb feeding off the Georges River.

'Where did you hire this...?' She hesitated to call it a boat.

'This gondola.'

Her laugh was immediate. It was partly fuelled by sheer joy at sitting across from him again. She hadn't realised until she'd opened the door to him earlier today how not-fully she'd been breathing in the previous six weeks. She sucked in the fresh air now and her body exulted. 'This is not a gondola.'

He ignored her. 'We're not going to get to Venice on a freighter and even hiring a gondola here was more costly than I thought was appropriate, given the no-money restriction.'

'This was the best you could steal?'

He tutted, offended. 'Make, actually.'

'You made this?' She stared at the most cerebrally talented man she knew. 'With your hands?'

He flushed overtly. 'I had help, but yes.'

In that light, it wasn't all that bad. But it still wasn't a gondola. 'Why isn't it finished?'

He stared at her. 'Because I'm impatient.'

Her heart flip-flopped. Had he been eager to see her? He could have picked up the phone at any time. Then again, no, he couldn't, not without saying much more than he would have been comfortable with. 'Impatient to finish the list?'

His eyes darkened and one side of his mouth quirked as he concentrated on keeping the little boat upright. 'No.'

Oh. But she wasn't brave enough to ask further so she worked her way around to what she really wanted to know. Crafty as a fox. 'Who helped you make it?'

'Russell.'

Should that mean something? 'Russell who?'

His dark brows folded down. 'Actually, I don't know. Russell from the dolphin place.'

She sat back hard in the canoe. 'The guide?'

'Yeah. He's a carpenter in his day job.'

Not a very good one, it seemed. But, since it was better than either of them could have done she wasn't going to judge. 'How do you know? You only said two words to him.' And neither of them were polite.

'We've been...working together.'

'What? Since when?' Not cool, that high-pitched squeak in her voice. She moderated it.

'Since about a month after we went out into the surf with him.'

She gaped and then grabbed at the sides of the boat as it rocked perilously again.

'He got me involved with the Dolphin Preservation Society. They're a client now.'

Umbrage broiled up fast. 'You hit them up for business?'

His lips thinned. 'Yes, Shirley. I figured they must have millions hidden beneath the moth-eaten nothing they appear to have and I wanted my cut.'

She let the rest of her confusion out on a hiss. 'I don't understand.'

'I work with them *pro bono*. Help them to position themselves in the market, to find contributors for their cause and customers for the beach experience. Building their capacity.'

A strange kind of mist rose on the water, swirled around their boat and then sucked up into her body, making her feel light and fluid. 'You helped them?'

'I am capable of random acts of kindness from time to time.' His words were half defensive.

'I... Yes, of course.' She'd seen that gentle side at work. Up close and personal. 'Why didn't you tell me?'

'I just did.'

'No, months ago... Why keep it to yourself?'

'I knew you'd carry on like this. Make a big deal of it.'

'I'm not carrying on, I'm curious.' She sat taller. 'And it is a big deal.'

'Well, far be it from me to fail to assuage Shiloh's fathomless curiosity.'

Super-hedge. And then it hit her. Her breath tripped over the skipped beat of her heart. 'Did you... Was it because of me?'

Ridiculous, surely. He wouldn't care what she thought of him. Beyond what she thought of him in the sack. And he knew the answer to that. Because no one could fake the responses he elicited.

'No, it wasn't for you.' Immediate. Slightly urgent.

Okay. 'So it was for you?'

He rushed to address that misconception, too. 'No, it was not. It was for them.'

She smiled as he realised he'd been snookered. Whether for her, or them or himself, it didn't change the facts. 'That's a pretty significant philosophical shift, Hayden.'

'You think I'm only interested in money? Ever?'

'Based on the evidence, yes.' Except now the evidence had changed. Now he'd thrown a massive curve-ball into her neatly stacked up preconceptions. And she knew she'd never be able to stack them the same way again.

Which meant it had just got a whole heap harder to keep her feelings at arms' length. While he was a man who would use his skills to exploit and manipulate others it was possible to maintain a rigid defence against the attraction and intrigue that battered on the door of her resolve.

But if he was a man who helped those who helped others. A man who'd carve a boat to please her. Or jump from a bridge...

She needed to move things back onto a safer footing. 'So this is our gondola?'

'And this—' he cast his arms wide at the ultra-modern canal lined with expensive houses '—is our Venice.'

It was a bit of a cop-out, but then again Venice was a very long way away, and he had *built something*—with his hands— for her. That was a turn-on in a very caveman kind of way.

Okay, Venice it was.

She settled herself more primly in the bow of the boat and tucked the folds of her skirt around her. 'Shouldn't you be poling us along? And singing in Italian?'

'Nobody needs to hear that,' he joked. 'But...*Ecco!*'

He drew a tall, brightly painted pole from along the floor of the canoe. The boat wobbled horribly as he rose to his feet, balancing the timber across him like some kind of trainee circus performer and then lowering it into the water on one side. Somehow they stayed upright.

'Is it long enough? This channel looks awfully deep.' It had to be for some of the enormous pool toys moored to every jetty.

He slid it into the water. 'We'll find out.'

It was, though Hayden's prowess in the field of gondoliering left a lot to be desired. Fortunately his prowess in other fields more than made up for their slow progress. They splashed on in silence for a few minutes and Shirley let herself enjoy the view. Both in the boat and out of it. Hayden's muscles bunched under his T-shirt as he propelled them along, his locked thighs holding him steady in the little boat.

She let herself look her fill. Everything around them went kind of...glazy.

'Don't look at me like that, Shirley,' he warned after a silent moment. 'It's just a canoe.'

Whoops. What had she failed to disguise? She caught his

eyes. Held them. 'You built it with your hands.' *For me.* 'That's not nothing.'

His snort was about as graceful as his boat. 'I did that to get laid. I knew I couldn't show up empty-handed and expect you to invite me back into your bed.'

No. She knew him well enough now. The defensive tone stood out in mile-high fluoro. He'd done it for her. To please her. A warm rush started at her toes and worked its way upwards. But pressing the point wasn't going to help matters.

'How kind that you were willing to wait for an invitation,' she teased.

He smiled, infuriating in its confidence and seat-squirmingly uncomfortable in its sexiness. 'Lip service. I know how I affect you.'

Yes, he did. More fool her. And he was affecting her right now. To the point that she wanted to do something about it. Something they weren't going to be able to manage in his terrible gondola.

So she changed the subject instead. Big time. Desperate times, desperate measures.

'How old were you when your mum died?'

Hayden dropped his chin, didn't answer, just kept punting them along. For the longest time. 'What makes you think she died?' he eventually said.

She shook her head. 'What you said just before you met Twuwu, about your parents sitting there together being the least likely thing you could ever imagine. And then at the gorge, you said that we were a decade too late for her.'

'It's not really something I talk about,' he said.

None of your business, in other words. She'd been telling other people straight for long enough to recognise *from the hip* when she saw it. And to accept it. It wasn't reasonable to be offended by it. Even if it also hurt.

'No. Okay.'

Splash, splash... They drifted on, a dark, heavy cloud suddenly hanging over Hayden. She distracted herself looking at the McMansions lining the canal side.

He cleared his throat. 'There was a reason I was so gutted when we lost your mum.'

We. She would have liked that sentiment at the time; it would have made her feel less alone.

'It hit me extra-hard because I was grieving for two mothers.'

Her stomach tightened. 'Did yours go that same year?'

'Three years before. Just before I started coming to your house on Saturdays.'

Shirley realised what a jerk she'd been, assuming his anguish at the funeral had all been for effect. 'You hadn't grieved?'

'Not properly. There were…reasons for that. But it all kind of caught up with me at Carol's funeral.'

Where did a girl begin to undo that kind of mistake? 'I'm sorry that I judged you for not starting the list.'

He shook off the dark cloud. 'Their deaths motivated me. It reminded me that you can't rely on anyone but yourself. I set up Molon Labe the next year. Started small, building a client list, making my own way.'

She stared at the darkening waters that rolled in huge swells past the boat. 'And your father?'

'He's still around. I see him about once a year when he wants money.'

Her chest squeezed as tight as his voice. 'God, Hayden…'

'It's a small price to pay. Literally.' He glanced at her sideways. 'What about yours?'

Her father? The man who'd left them when she was small. 'No idea. I don't remember him.'

Didn't let herself, anyway. Though she'd found a photograph amongst her mother's things and kept it. Just because.

'Carol only spoke of him once. Sounds like a man unsuited to settling down.'

A man just like Hayden? Was she really that much of a cliché? Falling for a man like her father? 'I wouldn't know.'

'You've never tried to find him?'

She looked up. Her chest pressed in. 'He knew where we were all that time. He lived there, too, when I was a baby. Until he left. And we were doing fine. Mum finished her PhD at night, then she went back to work as soon as I was at school full-time. We got by.'

'What about her funeral. You didn't send word?'

'I sent word.' She dropped her eyes. 'He just didn't come.'

'That's...' A lost-for-words Hayden was a rarity. 'He had no contact after he left?'

The pressing against her lungs became crushing. 'He'd made his choice. He left because of me; he was hardly about to ask for weekend visitation.'

Hayden stopped, turned towards her. 'Who says he left because of you?'

She studied the sparkling water. The poling stopped.

'Shirley?'

'He wasn't ready for fatherhood. And I wasn't a quiet baby.'

'But who *says* that?' He pushed them along again. 'If you were so young, how do you know that's true?'

She blinked at him. 'Mum said. Now and again. When she was mad or upset.' Or wanting to dent Shirley's embryonic spirit. 'Sometimes she'd talk about how much she loved him. Other times she'd talk about how he wasn't cut out for parenthood. Or how maybe if I'd been quieter...happier...'

'She blamed you for his leaving?'

'She *attributed* his leaving to me,' she said carefully. 'There's a difference.' But when you were six years old, the difference wasn't very distinct. 'It took her a long while to get over him.'

He shook his head. 'She never remarried?'

Shirley raised her hand. 'Guilty again. It was hard to find love with a toddler in tow.'

Hayden frowned. 'Where are these words coming from? They're not yours.'

She actually had to think about it. Though she knew exactly where the ideas had come from—and the words—when she let herself acknowledge it. 'My mother wasn't quite so prosaic when it came to her own emotions as she was when discussing Nietzsche or Socrates or Demosthenes.'

'And you were how old?' His words were as unexpectedly gentle as his touch late at night.

She shrugged. 'Depends; she said some more than others.'

But enough that she'd received the message loud and clear. Enough that Shirley had spent her young life trying to make up for crimes she hadn't even meant to commit.

He stared at her. 'My mother was far from perfect, but everything she did she did for me. I can't imagine her ever putting her own needs ahead of mine like that.'

The intense desire to excuse her mother overwhelmed her. That was straight from the ancient part of her brain. 'She was brilliant and focused and hardworking and totally dedicated to her job.'

To the exclusion of all else.

He turned and looked at her. 'I guess all that focus had to be coming from somewhere.' She glanced away. 'I'm really sorry it was from you.'

She shrugged. 'It's not your fault she wasn't better at the personal stuff—'

'It wasn't your fault either, Shirley.' He moved them onwards, visibly battling with something. He lifted the pole out of the water and sat down in front of her, with it lying flat across the gondola. 'I'm sure there are things in your childhood you *did* do and you can feel all the guilt in the world you want over those, but don't take on your father's abandonment. That's a reflection on him, not you. And if your mother let you be the reason she never tried to build a new family for you, then that's on her. Plenty of single mums build new families. Their kids are only an impediment if they're looking for one.'

'Why would she seek out reasons not to find love again?' Who *didn't* want to be loved? Other than Hayden.

'Maybe she couldn't find it and it was easier to blame something external for that.'

She stared.

'I'm just saying you shouldn't carry guilt for her issues,' he finished.

She sat up straighter. 'I'm not.'

'You're carrying something. Why else would you have this burning desire to finish her list?'

'To honour her memory.'

'Why does it need to be honoured?'

'Because I loved her.' Even if it wasn't a perfect love. She was the only mother—the only parent—she'd had.

'You don't need a bunch of activities to love her. Why the list?'

She stared at him. Utterly at a loss. How had their nice day on the water turned suddenly so very confrontational?

He wobbled back up onto his feet and moved them along again. 'That's a rhetorical question, Shirley. You don't have to answer to me. Only to you.'

They rowed in silence, the *splish-splash* of the pole becoming quite hypnotic.

'Amazing we turned out such a balanced pair, really,' he murmured into the warm air.

His smile was contagious. Then it turned to a chuckle and a full-out laugh and the gondola rocked. Neither of them could really claim any prizes for mental health. Not if you scratched below the surface. Not even far below.

Maybe misfits were drawn to each other.

'Take me back to the jetty, Hayden,' she breathed.

Jetty, car, her place. It was a one-hour trip, minimum. The sooner they could be in each other's arms, the better. And the list clock was ticking.

'Does that mean you don't want to see my place?'

She lifted her head. 'What place?'

'The house behind the jetty. It's mine.'

She twisted to peer down the canal the way they'd come. A huge beige monstrosity stood beyond an immaculate field of heavily reticulated turf.

'That's yours?'

In her periphery, she saw him nod. Watching her closely.

She turned back and folded her hands in her skirt and stared somewhere over his shoulder. 'I like the cottage better.'

He stopped poling. Stared at her. Then he slowly started up again and muttered, 'Me too, actually.'

'Though it is pleasingly close,' she teased, and plucked at the front of her peasant blouse. Loving the way his eyes instantly refocused.

'You want to see it?'

'You made me a boat—' she shrugged, all absent concern '—I suppose that deserves some reward.'

He turned the gondola and punted double-time back towards the jetty. Following the strong movements of his muscles gave Shirley a thoroughly good mental distraction from his innocent question.

She'd never asked herself why the list had become her obsession virtually the moment she'd discovered its existence. Why she'd ridden it hard through the past decade. Why she'd built her life around accomplishing it.

For a woman used to asking the hard questions, this simple one her stumped.

Why the list?

'Home sweet home,' he said, sliding the patio door open and letting her into the ultra-white, ultra-clean living area.

'No, it's not. You don't live here.' A house full of props selected by a stylist, maybe, but nothing *his*. No mess. No plants. No books. It was the latter that gave him away most—his cottage was overflowing with books. Stuffed into every available crevice. 'You probably bring women here. Maybe you stay here when you have late meetings. But you don't live here.'

'I did,' he murmured, reaching into the enormous stainless-steel refrigerator for bottled water. She got glimpse enough to know the only other thing in there was a long-life milk carton. Unopened. 'For quite a few years.'

She slid onto a white leather stool. 'When did you move out to the cottage?'

His hand paused on the steel lid of the ornate designer water bottle, then flicked it off carelessly. Its tumble clattered and echoed in the big house. 'Couple of years ago. When I scaled back at the office.'

'Why was that?'

'I needed time to reassess.'

Their lives were so different. The idea of just dropping off the grid for two years to *reassess*. 'And how did everyone at the office feel when you recently reappeared?'

'I took the front-of-house team to lunch. Made their managers sit on reception.'

She grudgingly smiled. 'I'm sure that was popular.'

'It got their attention. One coped just fine and the other knows where his knowledge gaps are.'

'And the receptionists?'

'Had a lovely lunch, got sloshed and betrayed everything that was really going on while I was away.'

Away. As if he'd been off travelling. Maybe that was what they thought. 'Their existence should be hellish once you start firing people,' she murmured.

He slid a glass of water towards her.

'No one's getting fired. I'm not going to punish anyone for something that was my doing. I was too focused on keeping the clients happy; I neglected the team. The people who helped me deliver it. So that's my mistake, not theirs.'

She stared at him for long moments, unease at discovering these new aspects to him fuelling her confusion. Working with NGOs, owning his mistakes, hand-making boats.

What was he doing—*trying* to be irresistible?

She shook her head. 'Who are you?'

'Maybe a better question would be "who *was* I?"' He leaned back on the kitchen island, tall and strong, his hips turned squarely towards her, ankles crossed. 'And the answer was "blinkered and self-involved".'

'Past tense?'

'Somebody helped me to see things a little differently. To widen my lens.'

'Would that someone be me?' She dropped her eyes, then glanced up at him.

He winced. 'See, *somebody* is bound to get full of themselves and become unbearable if I answer that.'

A smile slipped past her careful barriers. 'Not that you'd recognise the signs of that.'

His own lips parted in a reciprocal smile. 'Not at all.'

'Huh. Shame,' she said, leaning back as far as she could on her white stool and matching his body language. 'I find self-confidence extremely appealing.' He paused with the glass of water halfway to his lips. 'Almost as appealing as that whole bad-boy thing you have going on.'

But only because she was starting to understand it was just a mask he wore. Maybe only another mask-wearer would notice.

'I didn't realise the bad-boy thing was part of the attraction.' He placed his glass on the spotless benchtop and moved towards her. 'Being a jerk will certainly save me a heap of time and effort.'

She laughed and tipped her head up to face him. 'You've exposed yourself as a decent guy now. Damage is done.'

His grin turned feral. 'It's only just gone noon. I have hours yet to disappoint you.'

God, she adored this man's brain. She knew plenty of smart men who left her cold, so it wasn't just an IQ fetish. Hayden did intellectual foreplay like no one else on this planet. He barely had to try. No wonder she'd fallen for him.

She spluttered her first sip of water.

Realisation and despair flooded her in equal measures.

Hayden relieved her fingers of her own half-drunk glass and Shirley used the moment to curl her other hand around the leather top of the seat and steady herself while her world rocked. Like balancing in the gondola in stilettos. She kept her eyes fixed on him, convincing herself that if he wasn't stumbling then the intense rocking couldn't be real.

Fallen for him? Was she that stupid?

He helped her down off the stool and led her across the lower floor of the property. 'Where are we going?' she murmured past the tight choke in her chest.

Love. The one thing she'd promised herself she would not do. Not with him.

He turned back to her, oblivious to her crisis. 'I thought you might like to see the view from the bedroom.'

She forced air back over her lips and into her tight lungs,

determined to give nothing away as his fingers curled more securely into hers and they stepped onto the central stairway. 'That's subtle. Has that worked for you in the past?' She forced another breath in.

That was the key—in, out, in, out. Until breathing felt normal again.

'It's working for me now. You're still moving.'

She made herself laugh. Light and casual. Nothing like she actually felt. 'It's in my best interests to follow you. We don't have much time together. I wanted this.'

But she didn't want to love him. She hadn't meant to.

'See. You're an influence natural. I should recruit Shiloh.'

That actually achieved the impossible, distracting her slightly from the momentous bad news of just a moment before. The one starting with L…

She stopped midway up the stairs and stared at him. He turned back and looked down at her.

'It hasn't dawned on you yet, has it?' he said. 'How similar our jobs are.'

'They're nothing like each other.'

'Come on,' he challenged. 'You didn't write that article on Russell's group to get him a swag of new supporters? To raise awareness about dolphins?'

'I informed people…'

'You influence them.'

She stared. He pulled her into movement again, up onto a landing as immaculate and show-homey as downstairs.

'You appealed to their compassion or their intellect, you targeted it and you used it. Admit it, we're in the same game.'

'No, we're not.' He seemed way too pleased with that idea.

'I shouldn't be surprised; we were taught by the same woman.'

Fortunately, he stopped to open two enormous doors into an equally enormous suite. That saved her the trouble of having to plant her feet again.

'What?'

'Your mother was the queen of influence, Shirley. She knew

how to get the best from her students, the top grants out of her institution, the best office from her Dean.'

She had sure as hell known how to get her daughter to toe the line.

'Is this really your best effort at foreplay, Hayden? Talking about my mother?' But even that was better than the way her thoughts had been headed downstairs.

He swung her around in front of him to stand at floor-to-ceiling windows that looked out over the sparkling canal. 'No, this is…'

He pressed a button and they darkened just slightly. He moved up behind her and leaned her into the glass.

'One-way tinting,' he murmured, reaching around both sides of her to loosen the ribbons of her blouse. 'We can see out, no one can see in.'

Anticipation robbed every thought from her brain. And an empty mind was exactly what she needed right now.

An empty mind, a fully occupied body and strong arms to hold her.

Together, they might just be enough to outrank a heart gone rogue.

CHAPTER ELEVEN

HE'D finally got his fantasy moment there in his pristine white bed, unlacing Shirley hook by hook as though she were some medieval maiden, burying his hands in layers of fabric and stripping it back. Kissing the colour right off her mouth and revealing the pink, pure lips beneath.

The whole gondola thing had been a travesty. It had seemed like such a good idea at the time but he'd come across as a sap and a soft touch, telling her about his work for the dolphin mob. Thank God she hadn't pressed him regarding the growing list of others.

How would he explain that he had besmirched his soul in seducing her and now he scrubbed it clean again helping a raft of new clients? They bought him perspective. And balance.

A good balance.

He still struggled with the lingering sense that there was something extra *wrong* about the time he spent with Shirley; that it had just been too fast for him to believe she wanted this as much as he did, so it was probably just as well that weeks passed between them seeing each other. And it was probably just as well that the list was nearing an end for her.

A dark shadow took him.

He stared at *www.remembermrsmarr.com* on his laptop, at his own listings and at hers she'd added back when he'd challenged her to. Shirley had had a seven-tick head start even before he'd started trying.

He ticked off 'Hunt for a dinosaur fossil' on the live site. That only left the three unachievable ones. Everest, a grandchild and being touched again. It was odd imagining that his mentor—the woman who'd insisted that Plato's intellectual love was the purest—had secretly wanted to be loved again. Touched again. And all the while she'd had a small, vulnerable girl right there just *begging* to give her as much love as she needed. And to receive it.

But this dinosaur trip into the desert meant their achievable list was done. No more list, no more reason to be together. No more together, no more sex. No more sex, no more precious glimpses deep inside the mind and soul of the most intriguing woman he'd ever known. And if he was getting intrigued and habituated...

Probably just as well it was over.

'Hey.' Shirley pushed into their tent, two coffees in hand, looking earthy and radiant.

Nearly over.

He had one weekend. One last opportunity to be greedy. He wasn't going to wish that away until he absolutely had to. He hastily unchecked the box.

She sank down, cross-legged, next to him and passed him a steaming mug. 'Freshly brewed.'

Coffee only came one way on this expedition—hot and strong. But it had been months since he'd craved something fancier. Barista-made had lost its charm. Plain and strong would do him just fine.

'Thank you.'

She was back to being Shirley again, regular make-up and a more moderate selection of clothes without a buckle or hook in sight if you didn't count her laced-up trainers. He loved to spend time with this Shirley. Though he couldn't say he didn't love it when Shiloh made an impromptu appearance in their limited together time, too. The wilder the better.

'What are you doing?' She leaned over to glance at his screen.

He tipped the screen towards her. 'Visiting the list. You haven't updated.'

Her eyes briefly flicked to the corner of the tent. 'No. I'm keeping track in my notebook.'

He tipped his head. 'Privately?'

She studied the floor and then lifted green eyes to his. 'I think it should always have been private. It should never have mattered what everyone else was doing.' She took a breath. 'I'm sorry I pressured you into it. That was unfair.'

Her unrealistic expectations seemed like eons ago. And totally irrelevant now. He wanted to say *without that we never would have met*, or something equally corny. Wanted to, but he didn't. He reminded himself that the past months had probably been all the better for being temporary.

'Are you kidding?' He kept it light. 'If not for you, I would never have detached my retinas or frozen my butt off in the desert.'

She smiled. 'It's lovely out here, though, despite the cold. So incredibly vast. Can you imagine how much life is buried in ancient sediment here?'

The ancestors of eagles, enormous wombat third-cousins, a sea-floor full of marine fossils from back when the desert plain they'd pitched their tent into had still been ocean floor. The team had uncovered lots of ancient bones, but none of them dinosaur.

Yet.

The museum had willingly taken on two unskilled assistants for the long weekend and even been kind enough to find them tasks to do that felt meaningful. They weren't. Everyone seemed to know that but they were entirely prepared to fake it out of consideration for their guests. This time, no one knew she was Shiloh and no one knew that he was loaded. As far as the museum team was concerned, they were just hopeless enthusiasts.

We can always do with enthusiasm, the project director had kindly told Shirley when they'd applied. And she'd glowed. There was a lot to be said for kindness.

And for Shirley glowing.

'What time are they heading out?' he asked.

'As soon as everyone's caffeine ratio is optimum. Mornings seem to be expedition time and afternoons are for analysing results.' She rummaged around, tossing things onto her air mattress. *Their* air mattress, since it was a double and since they were back in 'list time'. Short grabs of heaven every few weeks. Little contact in between.

The perfect set-up.

Shirley's mattress pile grew. A spare shirt, camera, notebook, drink bottle, insect repellent, sunscreen. Everything a girl could need for a day in the desert.

'Be right back.' She bent and crawled out of the tent and he took the chance to watch. He'd grown really fond of that rear end really fast. He hooked the fly sheet with his boot and pulled it back to see where she went as he sipped his coffee. The latrine tent. Dug way out in the distance, necessarily.

His own pack was already loaded up so he grabbed hers and started stuffing the piled-up items into it as well as taking a couple of snack bars from the container she kept perpetually handy. The notebook slipped off the pile as he packed and fell open at an oft-thumbed page.

Her list.

He stared guiltily. Cross-through after cross-through mocked his still poor effort. She had thirteen of the fifteen items. Worse than he'd realised. She'd even crossed the dinosaur one off already.

His belly looped back on itself.

Hang on... Thirteen? When only twelve were achievable?

He traced the page with his finger and then slid to a halt at the mystery tick-box. He stared.

Be transported by a touch.

His first reaction was an insanely powerful surge of self-satisfaction. His touch had transported her. *His* touch. Impossible to know exactly when she'd ticked that but there'd been a whole lot of touching going on since their first night on the *Paxos*. Then the gondola day. And the previous two days.

And then...right behind the conceit came a wave of dread.

That wasn't the tick of someone who was casual about their time together. That wasn't the tick of someone who was content to let weeks pass between encounters. Or who'd be unfazed about moving on when the time came.

The wave of dread solidified.

That was the tick of someone for whom their encounters had been meaningful. Enough to tick a box on a list that had taken on religious significance for her. That tick meant something.

Not something...*everything*.

He shoved the notebook and pen in on top of the snack bars and zipped the pack up, then sat back and stared at the brown swirl in his cup. Was it a mistake to have let himself believe she was in the same class of woman as the others in his past? Easier, faster women. Or was it just blind wishful thinking on his part? Maybe he'd just seen what he wanted to see?

Wouldn't be the first time.

'Taking up reading coffee grinds?' she joked, ducking back into the tent. She saw her packed bag. 'Oh, thank you.' She threw it over her shoulder, bent and kissed his cold lips and ducked back out again. 'I'll see you by the truck.'

Confusion roiled.

Her demeanour was relaxed enough. Her kiss, easy. She wasn't fawning or clinging. In fact she'd just ditched him for more interesting people, as far as he could tell. Nothing about her actions betrayed the glaring tick in that very significant box.

Unless... Was she so desperate to finish the list that she'd thrown in a near-enough-is-good-enough tick? Or maybe she was a good compartmentaliser: *transportational* sex in one department and the real world in another. Or maybe she'd only slept with him in the first place to get the tick.

No.

Just...no.

He took a deep breath and tossed his remaining coffee out of the tent door. *Maybe* he was making much more of this than it was worth. Her actions had to mean more than what she wrote down in private.

In her notebook...

Which was virtually a diary...

He straightened outside the tent, and intercepted Shirley's

glance from across the campsite. It was a smile, small and private, much like any other she'd tossed at him on any of their adventures. Yet it suddenly took on so much extra meaning.

Was it the smile of someone harbouring a secret?

Was it the smile of someone trying very hard not to liberate a much bigger, more gushing one?

Was it the smile of a woman who knew that their time was very soon to be over? A weaning-off kind of smile.

Or was it just the smile of someone quietly excited about the day and trying to be cool in front of the experts?

Hell.

He snagged his backpack and hauled it out of the tent after him.

And *this* was why ignorance was bliss.

It might have been one of the coolest things she'd ever done but it was also one of the dullest. As one half of the least experienced duo on the expedition, Shirley couldn't have expected to be in charge of anything exciting and, to be fair, the scientists alone were doing their fair share of grunt work, too. They stood as a group at the base of sheer rock face in an ancient eroded gully.

'This was once a cave system,' the head palaeontologist told them, 'before it all tumbled in and wore away to become the plateau we see today. So there's a decent chance of finding a few bits of interest.'

Hopefully that was palaeontologist-speak for 'dinosaur'.

That helped motivate her as the hours passed and teams of them spread out over parallel search vectors and combed the desert floor, literally, for anything of note. At first the pressure of not knowing what might be 'of note' and missing something significant crippled her, but as hours passed with no one calling for professional opinions Shirley relaxed and let herself just drift, eyes firmly down, looking for anything that just didn't look quite right.

It gave her lots of time to glance at Hayden one vector over and worry about what was wrong with him.

He'd barely spoken to her the entire drive out here. Lots of smiles—carefully neutral and thin—but not a whole lot of substance. And they never reached his eyes. She'd surveyed the past few days in the same way they surveyed the ancient cave floor, segment by segment with a mind for the smallest out-of-place detail. He'd been fine for the first two days, as chatty as Hayden ever got, and focused on the stories told by the museum team of their past trips.

But come the dawn of day three and he had become a different man altogether, distracted, uncommunicative, hollow.

Anxiety burbled close to the surface. Why was her go-to response to assume something was wrong? That *she'd* done something wrong? Perhaps he had some kind of threshold for living rough and he'd reached it. Or three days was too much living out of tins and gas cooker coffee. Maybe he was more accustomed to finer comforts than he'd realised.

Those were all much better options than the lingering concern that it might be her.

Or *them.*

'Nothing?' she asked, loud enough that he could hear.

He glanced up. Shook his head. Then went back to studying the earth. Clearly still distracted.

She swallowed the little hurt and the frown and redoubled her efforts on the earth as she walked forward at a speed akin to continental drift.

Rock. Tussock. Earth. Rock. Earth. Bone… She stopped and bent lower, examined it. Nope—too bleached and surface dwelling for something older than a year. That much she had picked up from the professionals.

Tussock. Earth. Rock. Odd-shaped rock…

She paused again, bent. Gently dusted some dirt away from the edge of this particular rock. Rocks, she'd discovered, tended to be roundish or sharpish. A sharp rock with rounded bits in it was noteworthy. A rounded rock with a sharp bit in it—like this one—was equally interesting.

'Eric?'

She called their floating expert over. He finished marking a site several vectors away and jogged over to her. 'Whatcha got?'

She pointed to her feet. 'Weird rock.'

'Excellent,' he murmured, forgetting her presence already. 'We love weird.'

He dropped a circular frame around the rock and stabbed a small red flag into the earth nearby. He pulled out a sand sieve and started to trowel the dirt around the rock into it, shaking the balance free off to one side.

Her job was to continue onwards.

She glanced up and caught Hayden's sideways look. He returned his gaze to the earth.

'Is everything okay?' she suddenly asked, surprising herself as she started forward again.

'Yep.' He raised his eyebrows. 'Good.'

'Hayden, you're way too surly a human being to pull off a convincing "chipper".'

He paused to stare intently at the dirt and Shirley got the feeling it was faked. He struggled with something.

'This is our last list item together.'

Her heart emulsified into soggy goo. That he was keeping track. And that he cared. 'Yeah, it is. I didn't think you were aware of it.'

A dark flush stole up his neck. 'I have a numbered list to keep me aware.'

Oh. Right.

He cleared his throat. 'So what happens now?'

God. What a horrible place to be having this discussion. Forced to remain ten feet apart and surrounded by others with varying degrees of good hearing, including Eric, who was only a few feet behind her, albeit fully absorbed with the excavation of her rock.

She took a breath. 'What do you want to happen?'

'We sort of fell into it,' he said. 'I'm not sure how we fall back out of it.'

Fall back out.

She did her best not to stumble on the disappointment. He wanted to end things. Just when she thought they might have moved past the whole friends-with-benefits thing. Of course he did. Why had she expected any differently? Tightness in her throat translated audibly in her voice, but she'd be damned if she'd let him see how deeply she was affected. 'How do you usually extricate yourself from unsatisfactory relationships?'

He looked up.

She looked down.

'It's not unsatisfactory, Shirley—'

'Sorry.' She smiled thinly. 'Maybe I should have said "past their use-by date"?'

His lips thinned. 'Ordinarily, we'd have established that up-front.'

'So this must be awkward for you then. Most inconvenient.'

'Shirley—'

'Though we kind of did, right?' she barrelled on. 'While the list was ongoing we could be...ongoing.'

He frowned. 'And you're fine with that? Now that the achievable list is over?'

She tossed her head back. 'Sure.'

'Meet my eyes when you say that.'

She forced them to his. Glared. Could he hear Shiloh in her tone? 'Get over yourself, Hayden.'

His own narrowed slightly, clouded. 'Okay then.'

'You don't think this would have been a better conversation to have tomorrow? We have tonight to get through yet.'

'We've managed worse.'

True.

Behind her, a throat cleared. She turned and stared at Eric, confused. How could she have forgotten he was there? He held a partially hacked away chunk of rock in his hands.

'Shirley, I'm going to take this back to Dave at the van. I think you might have something here.'

Really? 'Okay. Bye. Should I just keep going?'

What an inane thing to ask. And why wasn't she more excited? Maybe she'd just found a species no one else had ever identified.

'Yeah, you should keep going—' the bearded Eric laughed '—maybe you'll find more.'

He whistled through two fingers and one of the team marked

their progress in the ground, then stopped scanning the dirt to meet him just outside the search zone and examine the rock. They hurried together to the van.

She turned back the way she'd been going. Hayden stared at her. 'What did you find?'

She shrugged. *'Dinosaurus shirleii.'*

He smiled despite himself and despite the tension of moments ago. Then it turned into a wry chuckle before he returned to ground-scanning, shaking his head. 'You're impenetrable, Shirley. Nothing touches you.'

Not if she didn't let it, no.

The day stretched out with a few promising finds, and then dinner stretched out with more than a few fascinating discussions around the fire afterwards. Her weird rock turned out to be more fossil than rock—a fifty-thousand-year-old middle toe of something called a Thunderbird.

'Dromornis stirtoni,' their project leader helpfully added. 'The biggest bird in Australia. Three metres tall.'

'Rare?' she asked hopefully.

'Reasonably common.'

Of course it was. 'And not a dinosaur?'

'About one hundred million years too young for that. But Stirton's Thunderbird was a contemporary of the woolly mammoth, if it's any consolation.'

Shirley was struggling to feel consoled by anything much at all this evening, but that piece of news did at least rouse a comment from Hayden, who'd been silent for the best part of the night.

'Are you saying that Big Bird and Mr Snuffleupagus were hanging out even in the pleistocene?' he said.

His dry question caused a moment of stunned silence amongst the learned group who would have been forgiven for believing up until now that he was mute, but then they burst into laughter. Even Shirley had to fight the twitch of her lips.

She didn't want to find him funny. She didn't want to find him clever or witty or sharp. Or still the most interesting brain in the room even when it was full of bigger brains. She did better when he was being surly and stand-offish. It was easier then not to love him.

She lifted her eyes and sighed. She didn't quite manage to cover the appreciation in her glance. Hayden's lips thinned.

Great.

She turned back to the conversation.

The moon climbed higher and then between one conversation and the next it seemed to cross half the sky.

'It's late,' the project leader finally said, tipping the last of his coffee in the fire. 'I'm to bed.'

Shirley glanced at their distant tent again and knew she'd have to return there eventually. Staying up all night had occurred to her, but she was already wearing every layer she'd brought with her and it wasn't keeping the cold out any longer.

She shivered even in front of the fire.

'Come on, Shirley. Let's get you warm,' Hayden said.

Let's... How cosy that sounded.

'I'm fine.'

''Course you are. For a snowman.' He stood. 'Come on.'

They left the lingerers to deal with the fire and headed slowly back to their tent. Every heavy footstep bought her seconds of reprieve. At last the moment of truth...

She turned to face him. 'So, now what?'

His brow furrowed as he lifted his eyes. 'Now we sleep?'

'Is that all?' Or was it just a euphemism?

He grew cautious. 'Do you want that to be all?'

No. But it had to be. 'You sound surprised.'

He stared at her thoughtfully. 'I believed you when you said you knew we'd be over after this trip.'

'I do know.'

'So I didn't expect our final night together to hold anything other than a vague poignancy of parting.'

Vague poignancy... That was something, right? She took a breath. 'It doesn't.'

Blue eyes challenged her. 'Liar.'

'I'm not lying.'

His gaze grew acute. 'Then why is tonight any different to any other night we've shared if it has no other meaning? Why can't I draw you into the warmth of that bed, the warmth of my arms and body, and farewell you slowly and thoroughly, like a goodbye should be?'

It literally hurt to push words past her constricted larynx. 'Because we're done. We decided that out at the ridge, today.'

'We confirmed this trip would be our last,' he allowed. 'We're not done until I drop you back at your front door.'

She stared. 'Seriously? Down to the wire? Just so you can get one more roll in the hay?'

'This isn't about sex.'

She snorted. 'Of course it is.'

'This is about *us* meaning more to you than something casual. Because if you truly didn't care then you wouldn't have any concerns about sleeping with me now.'

Every muscle squeezed. He was way too close. 'No. This is about you wanting to milk a good thing for every drop.'

And she'd been beyond foolish to ever set herself up for this.

His expression grew dangerously blank. 'You think I'm hard up for female company, Shirley?'

She'd never asked him if he was seeing anyone else. She'd never wanted to know. Because asking meant trusting his response and somewhere way deep down inside that she never looked she feared she couldn't trust him. Not with her heart.

'I'm sure there's a queue waiting for their chance at a rich, handsome man, no matter how damaged.'

He pursed his lips and nodded. Then he spoke. 'Casting stones, Shirley?'

To look at him—his casual stance, his even colour—you'd think he was supremely unconcerned by this awful discussion. But the vein pulsing high in his temple said otherwise.

He was bothered.

She just didn't know by what.

She held her ground. 'I'm not damaged.' Not to the same degree.

'Oh, please… Look at the extremes you're going to in order

to please a woman who's been dead for a decade. Your career choice. Your choice in men.'

'What men?'

'Exactly my point. And when you did finally relent to one, it's casual and commitment-free. You're hiding from the entire world one way or another.'

'Pot, meet kettle.' Shirley glared. 'For someone who hasn't left his cottage in two years or had a steady relationship *ever* you're very fast to spot deficiencies in others.'

'I know why I went underground. Can you say the same? Why hide behind the job? The crazy outfits?'

Really? Now even her clothes were a crime? She threw her hands in the air. 'It's fashion, Hayden. It doesn't mean I dally in self-harm or dance around naked in a circle of stones when the moon is in its zenith.'

'It's a mask. And it fits you so well you've forgotten you're wearing it.'

She locked eyes. 'I'm having *no problem* right now understanding why commitment-free seems attractive...'

'Come on, Shirley, ask yourself. Why do you do all of this? What are you protecting yourself from?'

She stopped, dead. 'What?'

'How many close friends did you have growing up?' he challenged.

The rapid subject change threw her. 'A few.' *Two.* Two tenacious girls who never had been able to recognise subtext. They stayed with her, no matter what.

No matter what you did to ditch them, a voice whispered.

Or maybe test them.

She frowned.

'What do my friends—' or lack thereof '—have to do with anything?'

'It's indicative of you avoiding opening yourself up to people. What is it that you think they'll find if you let them in?'

Insufficiency. Her mind immediately filled in the blank. Someone who is somehow sub-par.

Her bunching muscles forced her to shove that away and focus on the man in front of her. 'I'm confused, Hayden. A few minutes ago you were the champion of keeping things light, now you're criticising my lack of commitment. You can't have it both ways.'

Like white blood cells rushing in to swamp an open wound, excuses clustered around her vulnerable heart, making a prickly shield for it. She wanted to be sorry she'd ever agreed to sleep with him in the first place. But she couldn't. He'd moved her in too many ways. But she certainly could be damned sure it never happened again.

'This whole conversation is only reinforcing my decision to end things now,' she said as she started stuffing her belongings into her two backpacks.

'What are you doing?'

'Packing. I'm not staying here.' *With you.*

'Where exactly do you plan on going? We're in the middle of the desert.'

He had a point. She hardly knew the museum crew well enough to crawl in with one of them. The back seat of the troop carrier was looking pretty good at this moment. 'Not your problem.'

'Shirley—'

She spun around on him. 'I found a dinosaur fossil.' Or close enough. 'So the achievable list is now complete.' She flat-lined her hands in front of her. 'We're done.'

'You'll freeze out there.' His voice dropped. 'You can't leave.'

Damn him for being right. Her hand stopped, mid-stuff. 'I can't stay.'

'Why?'

Her chest rose and fell with alarming regularity. Why couldn't she be more like the women in his past? Why couldn't she just enjoy a good physical send-off? Why did she want tomorrow to never come?

'Because it feels wrong,' she whispered.

'You offered a no-strings, casual relationship, Shirley. I just took you up on it.'

Yeah, well...that was before her feelings had changed. Although... maybe they hadn't changed at all. Maybe she'd had them all along and just saw them clearly now. Because even though she had all the reason in the world to despise him right now, she couldn't help but be drawn to his sheer presence, still. It was galling.

Lord. Had she fallen for him that very first day? Or had she just never got him out of her system from when she was fourteen?

She lifted her chin. Tired of subterfuge. 'Are you really that much of a machine, Hayden? You have no other feelings complicating things at all?'

His face became a mask. 'That's not what we were about.'

'And so you won't miss me? You won't wonder what might have been?'

He didn't answer. But he looked like he wanted the answer to be *nope*.

'And will you still be doing that in twenty years? Thirty?' she prodded, desperate to even up the emotional score. 'Is that how you plan to end your days? Alone?'

His tan turned slightly sallow under the lamplight. 'If I play my cards right.'

'You don't want that.' Surely?

'Not everyone wants the picket fence.'

'Or do you imagine you don't have to worry about forever?' she persisted. 'Do you truly think that you'll exit this world early in a blaze of glory? Like Leonidas? Or will you just avoid any kind of emotional connection until the end?'

'That's the plan.'

She stared at him, utterly lost. Heartsick. 'Why?'

'Because it's what I want.'

No one wanted to be alone. Not really. Then a thought popped into her mind. 'You said you knew why you went underground a few years ago. Is it connected?'

'I said I knew. I didn't say I was planning on sharing.'

Her confidence shrivelled. She could have argued that, Lord knew she wanted to. But she was too tired. Tired of thinking about him. Tired of hurting. Her soul ached.

She went back to stuffing her bag.

'Shirley. We're adults. I'm sure we can share a bed without mauling each other.'

'That's not what I'm worried about.' She'd take his arm off if he made a move on her. 'Given how I feel right now, I can't promise not to suffocate you in my sleep.'

He laughed. He actually laughed.

Maybe he *was* a machine.

Her badly packed belongings weren't fitting in as they had on the journey out. She kept shoving them down into unseen air pockets. Jerky and strong.

'Okay,' he said. 'You stay here and I'll go sleep in the truck.'

She turned heavy eyes up to him. 'You think your freezing point is lower than mine?'

'Oh, there are people who would assure you that I'm already sub-arctic.'

'Here. You'll need this,' she grunted, and tossed a sleeping bag at him. He stumbled backwards half out of the tent to catch it like a marked football and then lifted bemused eyes. Had he not expected her to agree? She lifted her chin. 'Unless that was just lip service?'

A curious expression crossed his face and he backed fully out into the cold. 'Thanks.'

'See you in the morning, then.' She smiled brightly and then zipped the tent closed in his face.

And then sagged down onto the air mattress.

He was right. They were as damaged as each other.

To please a woman who's been dead for a decade.

Harsh, ugly words. But were they true? Was that what she was doing? Pleasing her mother? She thought back on how desperate she'd been to cling to something stable in the awful, disruptive weeks right after the funeral. The list had been like an anchor then, giving her something tangible to focus on. As though as long as the list endured so did her mother.

Then, as she'd crossed from child into young woman, as she'd trained for the gruelling marathon, she'd realised that it was more about *honouring* her—just as Hayden had pledged all those months before. The list wasn't going to bring her, or

Shirley's old life, back. It was just something she could do. And had continued to do to completion on principle.

At least she'd believed it was principle.

To please a woman...

She'd certainly spent the better part of her childhood pleasing her mother. Studying hard, doing all her chores without reminder, keeping out of the way when she had students around. Making sure her mother never had cause for complaint. Because she held enough things against her daughter as it was: her father's departure, her failure to find someone else in her life—

Shirley frowned.

—her inability to apply for exciting jobs overseas, her inability to move to a more upmarket district outside Shirley's school zone. Now that she thought about it. She'd cried-poor Shirley's whole life, despite having a crowded wardrobe and the best magazine subscriptions. She'd rarely gone out to dinner or the theatre or even a movie with friends. *I can't afford it* she would say on a sigh. *Not with Shirley's school fees.* Yet they'd been able to afford cable TV and a gardener and cleaner once a week.

She'd been fourteen when her mother had died. She'd only ever seen her through a child's eyes. And of course she saw an accomplished, popular, beloved teacher and mother. Maybe she would have seen a bad money manager if she'd been old enough to understand what she was seeing? Maybe her mother had actually been lousy at friendships and that was why she'd surrounded herself with a revolving door of students who adored her, but she'd rarely gone out with any of her peers. Maybe she'd been loath to give up the stability of tenure and her home to chase new experiences but hadn't been able to admit that to her colleagues. Maybe her husband had left because their marriage had failed, not because Shirley had been born.

Shirley stared at the fabric wall of the tent.

Maybe a whole lot of things weren't as they seemed. How many times had her mother used the single-mother excuse to disguise her own failings? And how many times had she willingly let those excuses settle onto tiny, anxious shoulders?

More important, how much of her mother's denial had she inherited?

Her stomach churned, just like it had when she was little.

She *was* still trying to please her mother. Every time she worried about the list, about doing it right, about doing it fast enough or slowly enough, about doing it the way *her mother* would have wanted, it was as if she were still here, judging Shirley's performance. Finding her wanting.

And she was still six years old, trying to make up for all the trespasses she sensed but barely understood.

Her mother hadn't been a saint or a legend or an oracle. She had just been a flawed human being who'd had trouble with friendships and taking risks and who'd used the nearest justification to excuse it. At the expense of her daughter.

Something shifted deep down inside her, clicked into place so perfectly and comfortably it could only be *rightness*. And, as though in shifting it had uncovered a tiny drain hole in her soul, years of hurt and bewilderment started to drip away, leaving a lightness behind.

Damn Hayden Tennant.

What else was he right about, then?

Did she hide behind Shiloh so that no one could reject *her* or find her thoughts and opinions wanting? Did she avoid forming relationships? She had a raft of online acquaintances and faces to nod and smile at when she met them at public events. Media she knew. Contacts she cultivated. People she liked to sit with at tables who all knew her as Shiloh. But no real confidantes. No one she'd feel comfortable calling up for a chat. Or drinks. Or a movie.

No one to call to wail that her time with Hayden was over.

No one she'd let see her without make-up.

Her father had left because she cried too much.

Her mother had blamed her for *everything* wrong with their lives. And then she'd died.

Trouble making friends.

Abandonment and judgement of one sort or another everywhere she looked.

Had she come up with as many clever life strategies as her mother to avoid having to engage with people? To avoid taking personal risks?

Had it made her crawl inside herself and let nothing out?

Shirley forced herself to her feet, turned off the lamp and crawled onto the airbed, still dressed.

But she had let something out. She'd fallen for Hayden, un-wound for him, incrementally. Given him a space for his tooth-brush in her heart. She'd found, in him, her intellectual match and maybe her spiritual match too. Two damaged people grasp-ing each other in the darkness.

Only she hadn't realised it was dark.

And he wasn't so much grasping as holding her at arm's length. Long, rigid, determined arms.

Deep sorrow congealed in her gut. And now he wanted out. Whatever he needed to make him want to stay, she lacked it. She'd thought this connection they had would be enough to ride out the obvious disconnect between them.

But it wasn't.

The high-tech properties of the sleeping bag did their job, slowly forming a warm blanket of air around her. Her muscles relaxed. Her goose bumps eased. Her eyes grew heavy.

Yet they didn't close. Not quite.

She stared into the thick black of the night around her and waited for morning.

CHAPTER TWELVE

Ziiiiiip.

The sound morphed, in her dream, into the long, teasing tug of a dress zip lowered by warm, exploring fingers. She wriggled against the pleasant sensation.

But then came a rummaging, a huff, a sigh, and those sounds struggled to find a logical place in her subconscious.

She stirred. Turned.

A dark shadow sat hunched in the camp chair in the corner of the little tent silhouetted by the high moon outside.

'Hayden?' It was only as she whispered his name that the memory of their conversation just hours ago returned. She stiffened.

'I'm sorry, Shirley,' he whispered. 'It's freezing out there. The truck's door seals are shot. I'm going to wait out morning here.'

In a chair? Wrapped in a sleeping bag? Watching her sleep?

She rolled back over. 'Suit yourself.'

Silence.

Then a heavy breath.

She rolled back over. 'Were you hoping I'd relent and let you in?'

His low voice smiled. 'Kind of, yes.'

If he'd denied it she would have left him there to freeze. But the smile she could hear in his voice said so much about his amazing ability to compartmentalise his emotions. He was who he was. It wasn't his fault he was built differently inside to everyone else. He hadn't invited her affections or been dishonest with her. He was just a leopard with very definite spots. Not at all interested in changing them. Not for her.

Plain and simple.

He'd only called things as he'd seen them.

She rolled away from him again but spoke softly. 'Fine. Get in.'

The bed lurched before she'd even finished the sentence and Hayden tossed the second sleeping bag over them both, taking care not to touch her. But his cold radiated every bit as much as her warmth and she felt it across the gulf of inches between them. She slid her leg across to touch him experimentally with her toe.

'Oh, my God, Hayden...!' She lurched up.

He was ice-cold. Hypothermic kind of cold. He flinched as though *he'd* touched *her*.

'I'm sorry...' he slurred.

She turned. 'You're freezing.'

'This is like some bad porno,' he said, his laugh constricted by the spasms of his chest. He'd gone past shivering to a place of rhythmic, full-body muscle contractions.

'You need to get warm.'

His shaking head rustled against the sleeping bag he'd hiked up to his face. 'I don't think that would be a good idea for either of us.'

She wasn't in a hurry to have him pressed up against her, either.

'Take the underneath layer,' she ordered, 'and wrap it around you like a cocoon. It's got my warmth.'

He did it and the shifting and tucking let in a whole lot of cold night air. Her goose bumps returned. But then he was done and he curled onto his side and let her remnant body heat do its job.

'You're so warm,' he murmured as her toasty thirty-seven degrees centigrade soaked into him from the high-tech fabric.

Her lips quirked and she rubbed at the gooseflesh. 'I was.'

He roused. 'Now you're cold.'

She pushed him back down. 'I'm not hypothermic. I'll make some more heat. Don't worry. Go to sleep.'

She turned away from him and scooted as best she could to

her side of the double bed. It really wasn't big enough for much separation, especially with him curled. But she understood why he needed to be. His body was protecting its vital organs.

In the silence, the time between his convulsive muscle clenches slowly lengthened. Then eased altogether. His pained sigh was a kiss of cold air on the back of her neck.

'Better?' she whispered back over her shoulder.

'Getting there.'

It wasn't tawdry. He was about as protected from any accidental contact as he could be, wrapped in a full-body sheath of goose down. But she wasn't going back to sleep either. He was way too close for that.

'Thank you,' he whispered into the darkness.

'You're a jerk, but you don't deserve to freeze to death.'

'No...' His breaths drew out and his words sounded close against her ear. 'Thank you for finding me. That day.' He breathed again. 'Thank you for saving me.'

Every muscle in her body paused to listen.

'I was on a path nowhere good when you pulled up to my cottage that day. I'd quit drinking but the whole downward spiral hadn't really changed. You forced me back out into the world and made me engage with it again.'

A deep ache started up in her chest. What could she say to that?

'I love doing what I do, but I don't always *like* what I do,' he murmured between tremors. 'I don't like the expression I imagine on my mother's face when I think of her looking down at me from above and seeing who I've become. I didn't like the look on your face when you found out. The judgement.'

She opened her mouth to apologise.

'That's not a criticism of you,' he whispered against her back. 'It's me. It's my choices. But you've shown me a way forward that I think I can live with. The road ahead is no longer a dark abyss.'

She lay in silence, understanding that he needed to do this. Fearing he'd stop if she spoke. Greedy to understand him better, even if it was their last night together.

'My parents split when I was sixteen,' he breathed into her hair.

Just *split*? That was less dramatic than she'd imagined.

'My mother finally found the courage to leave. He wouldn't let her go before that. Or me.'

Her heart squeezed. Domestic violence. Closer to what she'd imagined.

'My father told her she could only go if I stayed. Knowing she'd never leave me behind. That's what he traded on. Our love for each other. If she stayed, I was powerless. If I stayed, she was. But with her gone...' He swallowed. 'I made her go. I was nearly sixteen, close enough to independent. By then I could play him like a piano, keep myself safe. But I couldn't keep both of us safe at the same time.'

His cold-slurred speech tapered off and she wondered if he'd fallen asleep.

'She left you with him?' she risked, not wanting to break the spell.

'And set up on her own across town. But she didn't get all her bone breaks treated professionally. One of them grew an abscess and leached toxins into her system over a couple of years. Irrevocable.'

Shirley swallowed around the sudden lump in her throat.

'Those years of freedom were the best of her life, even though they were still so imperfect. I avenged her every day, manipulating my father and learning to despise how easy he was to play. I had him in the palm of my hand and absolutely no inclination to take care with what I had. Everything bad I learned about human nature I learned from him, one way or another. As education went, it was powerful.'

So were his words, confessed to the night and suddenly so close to her ear. A tremor skittered down her flesh.

'She died about the same time you started coming to my house?'

'Registering for your mother's class was the best thing I ever did. Without her, I would have assumed all people were like my father. But I did it because I thought she was someone else

I could play. A great brain I could challenge and best. A whole class full of students to be smarter than. That's who I was.'

She pressed her lips harder together in the shadows.

'Except she saw immediately who I was and she never let me best her. She was always a step ahead, in a way that lifted me up to her level. It challenged me to be better, not smarter.'

Would he admire his mentor so much if he knew what she'd done rather than face her own flaws?

'I'm hurting you, Shirley, and I can't forgive myself for that.'

'Because I am her daughter?' she whispered.

He stroked her hair. 'Because you are you. But I can't be who you want me to be, I can't turn myself into someone who can do forever. Not even for you.'

She wanted to rail, to point out that she hadn't asked him to. But this was goodbye; fighting it wouldn't change it.

'And I *would* hurt you again, eventually. I would take what I know about you and your feelings for me and use them against you. Because that's what I do as automatically as breathing. I exploit people's natures. You are so much better off far away from me.'

She smiled into the tent wall. Hollow and empty.

'"*If you love until it hurts, there can be no more hurt, only more love.*"' This time it was his turn for silence. 'Mother Theresa,' she finished weakly.

'You don't love me, Shirley,' he breathed after a long nothing. Tight. Uncertain.

She forced a smile to her lips, even though he couldn't see it. 'Do I get any points for not meaning for it to happen?'

A slight crack on the last word betrayed the tears that had started to roll in the darkness.

'Shirley…' He scooted forwards, pressed hard up against her. 'Please don't cry. Please.'

'I'm not crying—' she laughed '—I'm leaking.'

'I am *so* not worth your tears.'

'You have a very low opinion of yourself,' she whispered when she had control of her voice again. 'Or a very high one of my tears.'

He pressed his lips to the back of her ear. 'They're diamonds to me.'

The diamonds tumbled free like a spilled bag of gems, then. And Hayden held her as they fell. Hours passed that way, a lifetime. Or maybe only minutes. But, when she next opened her eyes, early fingers of light stole through the fabric of their tent and he was still there, curled into an S behind her. Still awake, breathing steadily into her hair. Stroking her.

'Open your cocoon,' she murmured. 'I need a skin memory.'

He did, silently. She pulled off her shirt. He stripped off his. And she squirrelled back into his embrace, his hot, hard chest against her back, his arms draped securely across her. They lay there like that until the camp started to rouse around them. She tucked his arms more firmly around her, so he could never leave. He pressed his lips to her shoulder and they'd warmed back up to his usual blazing-hot furnace.

'I love you,' she whispered to the morning.

Admitting it felt like the healthiest thing she'd ever done in her life.

He kissed her neck. Stalled. Then said gently, 'You deserve to have that love returned.'

Ache coiled up into a serpent in her belly. He found her lips and pressed his there, hard and desperate. She clung to them, far beyond caring what he might think or what that might say about her. Or how much it would hurt later.

This was their last kiss.

Deep inside, her heart tore away from the sheath holding it suspended in her chest cavity and it split open as it tumbled down to lie, askew, against her diaphragm. She pushed out of his arms and wobbled to her feet, clutching her shirt to her bare chest, unwilling to be as physically vulnerable as she was emotionally.

She stumbled across the tent. 'I have to finish packing.'

Hayden let her go. Watched her silently as she dressed and then stuffed some final items into her bag. Her pain reached out to him and twisted around his gut in eloquent agony. But, no matter how much she hurt now, this was still better than what he might do to her if he stayed. What he'd done to his father.

How he'd twisted him up in psychiatric knots. Until the day he'd walked out of the front door of the family home he would never see again, leaving his father cowed and intellectually broken.

Every woman he'd been stronger than, he'd controlled. He tied them up emotionally too, to keep them away. Just because he could. Because that was what he knew.

He'd gone on to ruin his monster of a father a hundred different ways through the clients he took on. To continue besting a man who could cause him and his mother no more pain. He greedily hoarded the fantasy that his finance clients would be foreclosing on Trevor Tennant, the insurance companies he consulted for would tie the monster up in loopholes, and the pharmaceutical company would have his father desperate and reliant on their products.

That fantasy made everything he'd done doable.

But it hadn't stopped him becoming the creature he'd fought. Controlling. A monster. Just like his father. Just in a better suit.

Behind him, Shirley spoke. Her voice was still hoarse from her tears. It rasped on his conscience like sandpaper. 'You're not packing?'

'I'll pack while you're at breakfast,' he lied. Hating himself just one more bit. Just when he thought there was nothing new left to despise.

She nodded sadly. Combed her hair. Left.

He let his head drop back against the mattress, let himself drown in her fast-fading smell on the pillow. The sweet, innocent smell of honesty.

No one had ever given him their love. Despite—desperately—not wanting to love him, she still did. One long-buried part of him held that to his gnarled chest like something precious.

He was loved.

Surely that was only a heartbeat removed from being able to love himself? Somehow? Some time? But letting her go now was emotional euthanasia. So much kinder in the long run, rather than prolonging her suffering.

Maybe it was something good he could finally do for someone.

Even if it felt bad.

Really, really bad.

'Hayden? The truck's warming up.'

Two vehicles were going back to the city that morning and two were staying to carry on the dig—the ones for whom being out here digging *was* their day job. Shirley's bags and equipment were loaded up in the first vehicle.

But their tent was still up. Surely Hayden wasn't going to just leave it for someone else to take down? She poked her head through the entrance.

He was back in his corner chair. Hands pressed to his thighs, waiting. The inside of the tent was otherwise exactly as she'd left it when she'd gone for breakfast.

Her heart lurched, then kicked into a hard rhythm as the penny dropped. 'You're not coming.'

Did the tent suddenly echo or was it just her ears?

'I think it would be better if I stayed a few more days.'

She'd been working herself up to the long silent drive back to the city, planning out her coping mechanisms, trying hard not to imagine how that final moment between them would go.

And here it was…happening live, in 3D. And she was totally unprepared.

Pain tore at her. 'So that's it? Goodbye?'

He stood. Stepped closer. 'I'll miss you, Shirley.'

She wanted to be brave. She wanted to be as strong and resilient as Boudicca. But she also wanted to curl up in a ball and die.

'No, you won't.' She knew that down to her marrow. 'You'll close the door on our time together before the dust plume has even settled on the horizon. That's what you do with things you don't want to deal with. You bury them.'

He said nothing. As though he would stand and take any emotional flaying she cared to dish out. As though that was what he was used to doing. That should have made it less satisfying, but it didn't. After everything they'd been through, all the excitement and clashes and intimacy, *this* was how they were going to part? So very civilised and…beige? In a tent?

No way.

'Say it, Hayden,' she gritted.

He stared at her.

'Say that I mean absolutely nothing to you. Say you don't love me and you never ever could. I want to hear it.'

His throat lurched. His eyes glittered. He didn't make a sound.

'Speak, Hayden!' she shouted and shoved at his hard chest, but a choked sob totally undermined her. 'I need to hear the words.'

His head tilted, his eyes creased. He gathered her hands into his and held them, hard, pressing his lips to them and speaking into her fingers.

'I will never be able to love you, Shirley.'

The air sucked out of the tent. She stared up at him, frozen. He held her eyes. He took her pain. He remained unmoved.

Outside, the truck horn honked.

Hayden gently released her hands and stepped back. She stumbled against his chair and glanced down to right herself. When she lifted her eyes he'd turned, robbing her of a final connection with those deep, expressive eyes. Gave her his back.

'Goodbye, Hayden,' she whispered.

She got out of the tent with much more aplomb than she felt. She didn't stumble once on the way to the truck, or as she hauled herself up into its backseat, or as she defied her shaking hands and shoved her seat belt into its fastener.

And she didn't look back.

Because she didn't want to know if he'd turned around. If he'd followed the truck with his eyes.

She wanted to remember the exact girth and shape of his turned back.

It would help her to hate him. And as long as she hated him, she couldn't love him.

The truck rumbled away and she sought refuge in the steady stream of conversation from the other passengers. But deep inside she was reliving her own conversation—the conversation from last night and early this morning. Their last.

Mother Theresa had it all wrong.

There was *always* more hurt to be had in love.

CHAPTER THIRTEEN

*www.shiloh.com.au—An open letter to my mother,
19th September.*

Dear Mum,
*I've done as much of your bucket list as I could. I've
skidded down a hillside clinging to a sure-footed stock-
horse, I've trembled with exhilaration atop the Sydney
Harbour Bridge and I've thrown myself off a perfectly
sound one in New Zealand. I've felt his music as Beethoven
must have, and the extraordinary mercury-leather brush
of dolphin skin against my body. I've dropped down the
side of a building and floated high above the world. I've
been marched across by penguins as I lay enraptured on
an ice-sheet and moved to tears by a touch more reverent
and gentle than I had ever imagined could exist.*

*I couldn't do everything on your list, but perhaps that
was always the point. That life fully realised is something
you strive for but should never attain. Because once you
tick off that final box, what is left to do, then, but wait for
your allotted heartbeats to run out?*

*Somewhere in my childhood I learned that love is
earned, not bestowed, and believing myself unworthy of
it—yours, my father's, even my own—has shaped my life.
But it has made me more determined than ever to believe
that there is a love out there—somewhere—that strikes*

like lightning. Because surely if love demanded perfection then none of us would ever find it. And if it is no more than a thing to be won via strategic campaign, then who amongst us would ever have the heart to try?

It has taken me weeks to accept that I am the apple fallen from your tree. I have avoided risk in my life every bit as much as you did and I've let the excuses become truth, every bit as much as you did. In protecting myself I've damaged myself.

Therefore, today, I step out of the shadows into full sunlight, naked and exposed. I hope and trust that the respect and commitment my reading community has shown to Shiloh they'll extend to the real me.

I am the silent child watching, breathless, under the stairs. I am the girl with no parents. I am the blogger behind the mask. I am the woman who loved.

I am...and always will be...your daughter, Shirley Marr.

CHAPTER FOURTEEN

A YEAR ago she could never have conceived of standing here, swathed in thermal clothing and yak furs, gasping for breath, minutes from the base camp of Everest.

Yet here she was.

She'd outed herself publicly a month after getting back from the dinosaur trip and published her mother's list, along with the letter to her. The outpouring of support—from readers and media and sponsors alike—had blown her away and, not long afterwards, a ticket had arrived courtesy of a local travel agent who wanted to help her finish the list.

I can't help with both of the final things on your list, the agent had written, referring to her mother's desire to hold her grand-child, *but I can get you to Nepal.*

Ten days of flights, buses, yaks and hiking later and here she was… Staring at the bright wind-tattered prayer flags so typi-cal of Nepal and the scattered synthetic tents of the climbers. Being practically carried by her patient, serious-faced guide.

Five thousand metres above sea level, all uphill. And they called this 'base' camp?

She lifted her eyes to the peak of the mountain. 'Holy Mother' to the Tibetans. Despite being more than halfway up it already, Everest only got bigger. Less imaginable. Getting to base camp had nearly killed her, even with the compulsory acclimatisation days midway. No roads, no tracks, just vague, invisible trails lined with rocks. She couldn't begin to understand what scaling to Everest's summit would be like.

The tents in front of them looked like acne—bulbous and out of place on the spectacular natural landscape. She laughed out loud at the image and her guide threw her the latest in many concerned looks.

'Rest,' he ordered and then thrust a flask of hideousness at her. An iron-based drink. Good for blood cells, good for altitude sickness. Bad for taste buds.

She could have gone to North base camp. That was accessible by road. But no, she'd had to do it the old-fashioned way. Ready or not.

And, in her case, definitely not.

She looked around as her guide saw to their trusty yak. She'd become quite fond of the matted, stinky thing that tootled along under the very small burden of her backpack, tent and food supplies. It finally dawned on her, halfway up the trail to base camp, that the yak was actually for her, if she passed out, so that her Sherpa could get her back down again without having to carry her himself.

She might have been wobbly but she was still, at least, on her feet.

And she was here. The entrance to Everest base camp.

Tick.

Something about being halfway up this mountain made her feel very close to her mother. And to God, though she was not a religious person, generally. Here, it seemed, she was.

Her breath came as shallow and tightly as ever, thanks to the altitude, and she did her best to only half-fill her lungs the way her Sherpa had shown her. But she'd grown accustomed, now, to dizzy spells and dark patches at the edges of her vision and to slowing her pace to accommodate the lack of oxygen in her blood.

'Shirley?'

She spun at the sound of her name. Pure instinct. Visions were something else she'd grown used to as her oxygen-starved brain played tricks on her but that was her first aural mirage.

Except that it wasn't.

Hayden stood in front of her, bright orange trekking gear, tan even darker than normal.

Her breathing escalated. The dark patches swarmed.

She reached for her guide on instinct.

And then she passed out.

Gentle fingers stroked her back to consciousness.

She opened her eyes a crack and stared at Hayden.

The real one. Not the Hayden of her walking daydreams. Or her fevered night dreams. Her brain wasn't so oxygen-starved that it had forgotten how to deduce.

She sagged. 'You sent the ticket.'

Played again.

'I saw your blog,' he said. 'I wanted to do something to reward your courage. It was the only thing I could do.'

'Most people would send flowers.'

He smiled and quoted her. 'I'm not most people. I had to find something far more dramatic and convoluted.'

Her wind-cracked lips turned up at the corners just a little. 'Figures.' She looked around. 'Where am I?'

'Medical tent.'

'Did you carry me?' Lord, please no. As if passing out in the first place wasn't unseemly enough.

'You had a yak.' He laughed at the horrified expression she couldn't mask. 'The altitude hit me hard too; I wouldn't have been able to carry you here.'

She struggled to sit up. 'So you slung me over the yak, butt waving in the air?'

'Pretty much,' he conceded. 'You're going to be fine, by the way. You just hyperventilated.'

'I don't care why I got here. I care *how* I got here.'

'Shirley…' He smiled, reaching out and tracing a loose strand of hair. The soft expression on his face spoke volumes.

Her outrage dried up. Her smile died. How was *he* even here? She asked him.

'I've been waiting for you.'

'You knew I was coming?'

'I knew you'd use the ticket. I hoped you hadn't decided on a lengthy tour of Nepal first. I nearly died when I discovered there are two base camps. Who knew?'

Anyone who'd done the slightest bit of planning? 'What if I'd gone to the other one?'

'I had spies along both trails. I knew word would very quickly spread of a lone woman trekking towards base camp. Besides,' he added, 'I figured you wouldn't do the easy one.'

So he did know her, just a little bit. She narrowed her eyes. 'How did you get here ahead of me? Chopper?' She knew him a little bit, too.

A dark flush crept above the pinched neck of his trek gear. 'Yeah. From halfway up. Greatly jeered at as I landed by the climbers.'

'So that's "how" taken care of.' She swallowed. 'Now *why* are you here?'

'I needed to see you.'

'You have my address.'

'I needed to see you far from home, somewhere magical.'

Her breath started to thin out. Was it the air again, or just her usual reaction to Hayden's presence? She took what passed for a deep breath in the highlands of Nepal.

'Why?'

He stared, glanced around to see if they were alone. 'Because…'

She waited. The first month of being away from him had been pure misery. Knowing he didn't love her. Knowing he didn't even *want* her enough to just tell her what she wanted to hear. The second month, marginally better and by the third month she'd made some decent progress on getting her life back on track.

Hence the Everest trip.

'Were you overdue to throw my life back into turmoil?'

His eyes softened. 'Is it turmoil—seeing me?'

She swung her legs off the side of the stretcher and sat up. Her head spun. She breathed back the nausea. 'Nothing I won't survive again.'

His gaze changed. 'I don't know whether to be proud of your courage or ashamed of myself that you need to call on it.'

She held her tongue. 'Why are you here, Hayden?'

'I missed you.'

Was he serious? 'Couldn't find a blonde?'

'Not sex, Shirley. I missed *you*. The moment you left the dinosaur campsite, the moment you climbed out of bed that day.'

'You turned your back on me that morning in the tent, Hayden. The message was pretty clear.'

'I didn't want you to see my face. And I couldn't look at yours again. At the pain.'

The first part stopped her cold. But the last part rankled. 'Don't pity me.'

He took her hands where they'd bunched into fists. 'I don't pity you, Shirley. I pity me.'

What?

'I'd convinced myself that the pain I felt that day was yours. That I was simply responding to hurting someone I cared about.' He resettled himself on his haunches. 'But it went on. And on. And it finally dawned on me that it was *my* pain. I'd never been in pain before.'

'Everyone feels pain.'

'Not if you've numbed yourself to survive. I'd never let myself care enough, be engaged enough, be emotionally invested enough to care if something was taken away from me. Not since I was a boy. I'd shoved it right down deep inside out of sheer survival. I'd forgotten what loss felt like.'

Every humane cell in her body responded to that, totally overruling her anger.

'I don't want to be like him, Shirley. Controlling others to make up for something in myself.'

'You're not like him.'

'Two years ago it finally dawned on me what I was becoming. The socially acceptable version of him. So I dropped out and tried to get myself sorted. I thought I had it beat. And then you looked at me that day in the tent the way my mother used to look at him. That awful mix of pain and love and resignation. And I knew I was kidding myself thinking I could manage it alone.'

Alone. Was he looking to her to be some kind of salvation?

'I'm getting professional assistance now.'

Nothing he could have said—nothing—could have surprised her more. Not if he stood on the top of Everest and declared undying passion for her yak. 'You're in therapy?'

'He's an idiot—' he brushed it off, shifting the angle of his crouch by her stretcher '—but he seems to know some things. We're making progress.'

Given his budget, he probably had the best the country had to offer.

'But I didn't need Sigmund Freud to tell me why I was hurting. I missed you, Shirley. In my life. In my arms. In my business.'

He smiled, but she couldn't match it. This was all too monumental.

Seriously, if she woke up on the side of some pebbly track with her Sherpa and the yak staring down at her she was going to just...walk off the edge of the nearest crevasse. And have a very unfriendly discussion with the God she was starting to get a sense of up here.

She got to her feet and he pushed himself up to stand in front of her. She stared up at him. Made herself say it. The bitterest pill.

'You told me you could never love me.'

He dropped his eyes. 'I told you I'd never be *able* to love you. Not the way you deserve. Not the way it is supposed to be.'

It was impossible to know whether it was just *her* air that got tighter or the altitude. 'You let me believe it was me.'

'I thought that was what you wanted to hear. Needed to hear.'

He was right. She had. She'd needed to hate him. She lifted her eyes and took a breath. 'It's too late, Hayden. I've moved on.'

His dark brows dropped. 'On? To what?'

That was the problem with lying; ideally, you needed to have put thought into it. 'On to...getting over you.' *Ugh. Lame.* 'I'm going to hold out for someone who can love me the way I need, the way I deserve.'

His colour dropped slightly. But then his eyes narrowed. 'No. You fainted when you saw me.'

Confident words, but they weren't matched by his tone.

'It was the—'

'No, it wasn't.' Stronger. Surer. He shuffled closer. 'It was me. You still care.'

She clamped her lips together.

'Shirley, you're not that inconstant. And you're too moral. You might have been *trying* to get over me, but you're not.'

Pfff… 'You're so arrogant.'

He smiled. 'Yet you still love me.'

She dropped her head and when she lifted it she left behind all her masks, all her pretensions. 'Is this fun for you, Hayden, tormenting me? Is the ego stroke worth flying across the world for?'

His smile evaporated, his eyes darkened. 'No, Shirley. This is not about my ego. This is about my…feelings. My heart.'

The discomfort was what gave him away. It showed in every crease and fold in his handsome face. Talking about this was excruciating for him.

He was serious…

'Just say it, Hayden.' Whatever he'd come here to say.

He looked around them again. 'Not here. This is not how I imagined it.'

'No. Here, or not at all. You don't get to orchestrate every moment to your personal satisfaction.' Not when it hurt this much.

Indecision flitted across his features. 'Please, Shirley. Just step outside. Only a few feet.'

The plea was so honest and so earnest, it was hard to ignore. *Fine.* 'Just outside. No further.'

He led her out into the bright daylight. After the darkness of the tent, the electric-blue sky half blinded her. She raised her hands to let her eyes adjust more slowly. It didn't help when he turned her so that she was looking at him against the backdrop glare of the main peak of 'Holy Mother'.

'I need sunglasses—' she started.

'God, woman, you're making this very hard.'

His tone clamped her mouth shut. He'd never, *ever* snapped at her like that, hissing with frustration. Even when they were fighting. But, for once, she didn't immediately assume responsibility. Not everything was her fault. And that was a massive mental shift for her.

'Just let me do this,' he gritted. He paused, composed himself and then lifted his eyes back to hers. 'Shirley... You were never going to be just casual for me. I was a fool not to see it coming. I was way too fascinated and intrigued by you.'

Everest disappeared. Her entire vision right now—her entire world—was Hayden Tennant.

'I pushed you away and threw the gift of your love back in your face rather than face my own demons.' He blew out a long breath. 'I was terrified that I would hurt you even more if I stayed in your life. I even justified it that way to myself and felt quite the hero for doing the hard thing. I couldn't have been more patronising if I'd tried. The truth is...'

He frowned and struggled with what came next but she couldn't move for all the oxygen bound up in the snow-caps.

'The truth is, I was scared to let myself feel. To care. Love and I don't have a particularly good track record; my father's obsession with my mother destroyed her, my love for her imprisoned me with him. I have no idea what loving someone safely entails. I was frightened that I would stuff it up if I tried. That I'd fail and you'd end up hating me. But you ended up hating me anyway—'

'No, I didn't,' she murmured.

'You must have.'

'I wanted to, believe me. I couldn't forgive you but I couldn't forget you, either.' She sighed. 'And I couldn't hate you.'

His Adam's apple bungeed a few times. 'Then I saw your blog and what you said about not having the heart for a love that was like a military campaign—'

'Actually, that was—'

'Will you stop interrupting?' he barked. 'I'm trying to tell you I love you.'

Oxygen-less air whooshed into her lungs.

Hayden snapped his mouth shut, and then his lips tightened. 'Though I was hoping to do it more romantically than that,' he muttered.

She didn't dare breathe out in case there was nothing left to take back in. The dark patches appeared in her peripheral vision again. 'More romantic than at the foot of Everest? Having flown halfway around the world and paid off half of Nepal and Tibet to find me?'

His lips twisted. 'Yeah. More than that.'

She finally inhaled. A ridiculous lightness—totally different to what she'd felt coming up the mountain—suffused her.

His eyes darkened. 'This is what I came to. Love liberates, it doesn't entrap. It's not something you can plan for or manage. It's like stepping off a bridge into nothing.' He took a deep breath. 'But it's so much less terrifying when there's someone there, stepping off with you.'

She swallowed back tears. She'd done enough blubbing in front of Hayden for a lifetime. He took her hands.

'If this isn't love,' he said, threading his fingers through hers and boring into her with the intensity of his gaze, 'then it should be.'

So much for not blubbing. Tears spilled, heedless of her will, over her lashes and ran down her wind-whipped, make-up-less face. Lord, what a picture she must present. But she didn't care. She'd bare her whole soul if he asked her to.

And then—despite every fear and doubt and heartbreak and agony of the past months—they were kissing again. The sensation she'd believed she'd never have access to again, the rush of adrenalin that came from just touching him, coursed through her blood where the oxygen couldn't go.

She clung to his strong frame, weakened, and he gathered her more tightly in to him, worshipping her mouth with his. There was barely enough oxygen to go around for one, let alone keep two hearts pumping. They fell apart, panting.

'I am good enough for you,' she gasped. It felt important to make that clear.

He blinked, confused. 'I agree.'

'I mean that I'm through with doubting myself. Believing myself unworthy. I want a strong, equal relationship.'

'Princess, you're preaching to the choir...'

'And I want you to admit that this wasn't strategic. Neither one of us *made* the other love us.'

His eyes softened. 'Everything about you made me love you, Shirley.'

She glared at him.

'You want the lightning bolt?'

'I want you to admit that something special happened here. Something bigger than both of us.'

'How about I tell you when it happened, instead?'

She stared.

'I first bought in to loving you when you stood on my porch and called me an ass that day. No one had challenged me like that, ever.' He stepped closer. 'Then when your ridiculous stockings at the beach forced such lightness into the darkness inside me.' His hand twisted up into her hair. 'Then when you gave up your seats at the symphony for some strangers way up the back and you revealed your soul.'

Her eyes brimmed over again.

'But I still wavered. Then you were so natural and good with the boys at Tim's party and all I could think about was what a spectacular mother you would make.'

A tear wobbled free.

'But if you want the thunderbolt. The moment I knew I was screwed?'

Only from Hayden would she take *screwed* as a compliment. She nodded and shook another tear loose.

'The giraffe. That moment surrounded by sea containers and diesel fumes when you held your hand out to me, your eyes filled with such magic and mystery and drew me into your fantasy. No-one had ever given me the gift of joy before. Unconditional generosity.'

And there was the magic word.

Unconditional.

'I don't ever want to have to earn your love,' she whispered.

He stepped back and regarded her gravely. Then he sank to one knee, on the rocks and shale underfoot, just as he had inside the tent. It wasn't a proposal. It was older and more classic than that. It was a Spartan honour pledge.

'I give it to you. As a gift. Whether you want to keep it or not, it doesn't change how I feel. My love is yours, unconditionally.'

She sank down onto her knees to join him. The stones cut into her skin. She ignored it. 'I accept. And I love you. Every part of you.'

They fell forward into each other's lips, kissed as if it were their first time. Then they pulled back and stared at each other, lost. Panting.

'I caught up to you on the list,' he got out between breaths.

She leaned against him. 'In just a few weeks? How?'

'I cheated.' He laughed. 'We're neck and neck now that we're both here.'

She smiled. 'You know what? That list doesn't seem so important now.'

He curled his arms around her. 'Typical. Just as defeat is on the horizon.'

She chuckled. 'We have something much more impressive on the horizon.'

They stared up at the Himalayan peaks together. Awed.

'This really hurts,' Shirley finally admitted.

'You're not kidding.' He pushed to his feet and then pulled her carefully up with him off the sharp rocks.

'You know you're hiking down off the mountain with me, right? I won't be seen in your chopper.'

'And miss all those nights in a tent with you?' He kissed her again. 'I wouldn't have it any other way. You still owe me from the dinosaur dig.'

'We can't do anything.' She giggled. 'We'll have a guide sleeping just feet away.'

He pushed back and stared at her. 'Did you just...giggle?'

Truly unmasked now. Exactly how she wanted to stay. 'That's just one of a range of ordinary-person sounds I make when I'm not on guard,' she joked. 'And you're going to get to discover them all.'

He swooped down to kiss the side of her throat. 'That's not going any way to preserving the modesty of your guide. Now all I can think about is getting you in a tent and eliciting all those sounds.'

'Truly,' she said, curling her head and seeking out his lips for more oxygen deprivation. 'They can't be any worse than the sound of the yak on the way up.'

EPILOGUE

Two years later

EXACTLY as Hayden had promised her all those adventures ago at Everest, it *was* so much less terrifying when there was someone there, stepping out into the nothingness with you.

He hadn't left her side, not for one overwhelming moment of the birth.

She lay curled around their tiny baby boy, throbbing with love for this precious, precious gift. She'd thought it impossible to feel more love than she already did for her complex, brave Hayden but this little bundle had come out with masses more all ready to go.

She stroked his tiny cheek and glanced at her sleeping husband.

Hayden had pulled a chair up to the side of the bed and leaned forward to watch his son nurse with all the pride and amazement and trepidation of a first-time dad. Then he'd fallen asleep there, totally destroyed by the past forty hours, with one hand on her and one on his new son, draped on the side of her bed. Even the visiting nurses worked quietly around him so that he could sleep.

Then again, he had charmed every one of them. They would have done anything for him. She bundled Leo up more tightly in her hold and looked up and around her, too shattered—too happy—to sleep.

'Mum,' she whispered to the night. 'This is your grandson,

Leonidas. I'm sorry you can't hold him yourself but Hayden and I will hold him for ever for you and keep him safe.'

She stroked his flushed little cheek with her index finger. 'I get it now, Mum. How unprepared we all are at this moment. How much we want to be the perfect parent for our babies. But it doesn't change us. It can't make us perfect, or even better. We can only do our best.'

She gently extracted the sleeping baby from under Hayden's touch, bundled him more securely and curled him into a hold close to her body.

And then she rocked him and told him all about his grandma. *Tick.*

* * * * *

Mills & Boon® Hardback

November 2012

ROMANCE

A Night of No Return	Sarah Morgan
A Tempestuous Temptation	Cathy Williams
Back in the Headlines	Sharon Kendrick
A Taste of the Untamed	Susan Stephens
Exquisite Revenge	Abby Green
Beneath the Veil of Paradise	Kate Hewitt
Surrendering All But Her Heart	Melanie Milburne
Innocent of His Claim	Janette Kenny
The Price of Fame	Anne Oliver
One Night, So Pregnant!	Heidi Rice
The Count's Christmas Baby	Rebecca Winters
His Larkville Cinderella	Melissa McClone
The Nanny Who Saved Christmas	Michelle Douglas
Snowed in at the Ranch	Cara Colter
Hitched!	Jessica Hart
Once A Rebel...	Nikki Logan
A Doctor, A Fling & A Wedding Ring	Fiona McArthur
Her Christmas Eve Diamond	Scarlet Wilson

MEDICAL

Maybe This Christmas...?	Alison Roberts
Dr Chandler's Sleeping Beauty	Melanie Milburne
Newborn Baby For Christmas	Fiona Lowe
The War Hero's Locked-Away Heart	Louisa George

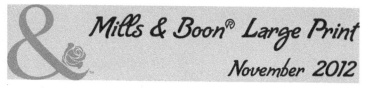

ROMANCE

The Secrets She Carried	Lynne Graham
To Love, Honour and Betray	Jennie Lucas
Heart of a Desert Warrior	Lucy Monroe
Unnoticed and Untouched	Lynn Raye Harris
Argentinian in the Outback	Margaret Way
The Sheikh's Jewel	Melissa James
The Rebel Rancher	Donna Alward
Always the Best Man	Fiona Harper
A Royal World Apart	Maisey Yates
Distracted by her Virtue	Maggie Cox
The Count's Prize	Christina Hollis

HISTORICAL

An Escapade and an Engagement	Annie Burrows
The Laird's Forbidden Lady	Ann Lethbridge
His Makeshift Wife	Anne Ashley
The Captain and the Wallflower	Lyn Stone
Tempted by the Highland Warrior	Michelle Willingham

MEDICAL

Sydney Harbour Hospital: Lexi's Secret	Melanie Milburne
West Wing to Maternity Wing!	Scarlet Wilson
Diamond Ring for the Ice Queen	Lucy Clark
No.1 Dad in Texas	Dianne Drake
The Dangers of Dating Your Boss	Sue MacKay
The Doctor, His Daughter and Me	Leonie Knight

Mills & Boon® Hardback

December 2012

ROMANCE

A Ring to Secure His Heir	Lynne Graham
What His Money Can't Hide	Maggie Cox
Woman in a Sheikh's World	Sarah Morgan
At Dante's Service	Chantelle Shaw
At His Majesty's Request	Maisey Yates
Breaking the Greek's Rules	Anne McAllister
The Ruthless Caleb Wilde	Sandra Marton
The Price of Success	Maya Blake
The Man From her Wayward Past	Susan Stephens
Blame it on the Bikini	Natalie Anderson
The English Lord's Secret Son	Margaret Way
The Secret That Changed Everything	Lucy Gordon
Baby Under the Christmas Tree	Teresa Carpenter
The Cattleman's Special Delivery	Barbara Hannay
Secrets of the Rich & Famous	Charlotte Phillips
Her Man In Manhattan	Trish Wylie
His Bride in Paradise	Joanna Neil
Christmas Where She Belongs	Meredith Webber

MEDICAL

From Christmas to Eternity	Caroline Anderson
Her Little Spanish Secret	Laura Iding
Christmas with Dr Delicious	Sue MacKay
One Night That Changed Everything	Tina Beckett

ROMANCE

Contract with Consequences	Miranda Lee
The Sheikh's Last Gamble	Trish Morey
The Man She Shouldn't Crave	Lucy Ellis
The Girl He'd Overlooked	Cathy Williams
Mr Right, Next Door!	Barbara Wallace
The Cowboy Comes Home	Patricia Thayer
The Rancher's Housekeeper	Rebecca Winters
Her Outback Rescuer	Marion Lennox
A Tainted Beauty	Sharon Kendrick
One Night With The Enemy	Abby Green
The Dangerous Jacob Wilde	Sandra Marton

HISTORICAL

A Not So Respectable Gentleman?	Diane Gaston
Outrageous Confessions of Lady Deborah	Marguerite Kaye
His Unsuitable Viscountess	Michelle Styles
Lady with the Devil's Scar	Sophia James
Betrothed to the Barbarian	Carol Townend

MEDICAL

Sydney Harbour Hospital: Bella's Wishlist	Emily Forbes
Doctor's Mile-High Fling	Tina Beckett
Hers For One Night Only?	Carol Marinelli
Unlocking the Surgeon's Heart	Jessica Matthews
Marriage Miracle in Swallowbrook	Abigail Gordon
Celebrity in Braxton Falls	Judy Campbell

Discover Pure Reading Pleasure with

Visit the Mills & Boon website for all the latest in romance

Buy all the latest releases, backlist and eBooks

Find out more about our authors and their books

Join our community and chat to authors and other readers

Free online reads from your favourite authors

Win with our fantastic online competitions

Sign up for our free monthly eNewsletter

Tell us what you think by signing up to our reader panel

Rate and review books with our star system

www.millsandboon.co.uk

 Follow us at twitter.com/millsandboonuk

 Become a fan at facebook.com/romancehq

PYRIDINE AND ITS DERIVATIVES

SUPPLEMENT IN FOUR PARTS
PART THREE

This is the fourteenth volume in the series
THE CHEMISTRY OF HETEROCYCLIC COMPOUNDS

THE CHEMISTRY OF HETEROCYCLIC COMPOUNDS

A SERIES OF MONOGRAPHS

ARNOLD WEISSBERGER and EDWARD C. TAYLOR

Editors